G000049351

TALESPIN

TALESPIN

Dear Barbara,

Thank you for looking after our daughter.

Nickunj Malik

Hope you enjoy the book.

Nickunj

JAN 2015

Ocean Books Pvt. Ltd.

ISO 9001:2008 Publishers

Published by
Ocean Books (P) Ltd.
4/19 Asaf Ali Road,
New Delhi-110 002 (INDIA)
e-mail: info@oceanbooks.in

ISBN 978-81-8430-315-5
Talespin
by Nickunj Malik

Edition
First, 2015

Price
Rs. 450.00 (Rupees Four Hundred Fifty only)
US$ 20 (US Dollars Twenty only)

© Reserved

Printed at
R-Tech Offset Printers, Delhi

for
my father, Satya;
my mother, Neer;
Micky and Icka

truth, love, laughter, kindness
~ you taught me the magic of life

Foreword

Reading a collection of Nickunj (the name means 'abode of love' in Sanskrit) Malik's columns is like living a second life. I don't mean, even in a metaphoric or ironic sense that I play the part of Lazarus and she of the Messiah. Engaging with her concerns is, for me, like being someone else. Let me count the ways: I don't live all over the world, I don't have domestic servants wherever I go, that is if I go anywhere, I have no prospect of meeting Popes and potentates, I have no relationship to motherhood, I am not attended by various medical consultants and physicians for real and imagined ailments and yes, though I do wear spectacles I never push them absent-mindedly to the top of my forehead and look all over the house for them…. I could go on.

The act of reading is in all instances an entry into another world. A primer in astrology, quantum physics, relativity or the mysteries of genetics takes us into a world we don't in the normal run of things imagine. Reading story-tellers such as Kafka or Jorge Luis Borges can take us into states of being or perception filled with wonder and the compulsion to indulge the imagination. The famous critic F.R. Leavis formulated the simple idea that great literature acquainted us, when the injunctions of religion failed to, with the possibilities of life.

Nickunj's columns do none of these things. They acquaint you instead with a whole personality, its meditations, quirks, worries, preoccupations, duties, meanderings, family life, the small crises of a household, the argumentative, comically and forgivably-vain conceits of characters she lives with and meets – with life as it is lived by Nickunj.

In the pages that follow, the collected columns written over several years, you meet Nickunj, as lively a character as any you will encounter in Dickens and you may appreciate the perspective on day-to-day life that provides the substance of her writing. This view is not endowed with the peculiarities of Picasso or the puzzles and traps for perception that Escher sets (you see I drop names, Nickunj doesn't!). It is rather, in the end, an expression of a personality concerned with everyday life, its simplicities such as a visit to the dentist and its profundities such as the nature of motherhood. Nickunj doesn't give us a thesis on the abstraction of maternity, she tells us about her mother and about being a mother herself.

For me, her strongest and most poignant writing is when she recollects her childhood and remembers and pays literary tribute to her father, mother and even in passing to her teachers and the nuns who didn't think that 'flu, or its symptoms – a runny nose, a fever and a body ache – were enough to excuse her from lessons though they were deemed sufficient to stay away from PE.

Ms. Malik tells us, and it came as something of a surprise to me as I read the columns in the order they were presented, of her childhood in which she wore dresses that were hand-me-downs from her older cousin sisters and about the frocks that her mother would stitch and which her brothers would be enjoined to preserve from dust and any danger of tearing and soiling when she tried them on.

There are in these pages refreshing pieces of journalistic description as when Pope Francis visits Amman and our writer is in the audience that greets him, engaging in details with the event and in some concern with the sun that's working at her skin tan. She concludes her lucid description with the speculation that there may have been some spiritual projection in Pope Francis' presence and speech, which transmitted benevolence, as the surly security officers who had greeted her sullenly at entry were doves of goodwill at her exit.

There are her encounters with Nelson Mandela, which are more vivid than worshipful. The first meeting involves Mandela coming in person, rather than summoning a servant into his presence through an apparatchik, to thank the man who has ironed his shirts that morning. The second encounter that the writer recalls with the great man is in a shopping mall when she and her family are transferred to South Africa. He... oh well! Read the piece it can't be better said.

The journalistic columns with this human touch leave me, without detracting from the allure of the other genres, wanting more.

I can't sign off from this foreword without an allusion to assortments of opinion and writing, which in this generation are transmitted through the 'blog'. (I think the ugliness of the word is appropriate, like the devil being called Beelzebub!). The ether is crowded with the vanity of unsolicited opinions. This collection is distinctly not from the blogosphere and in that sense, cherishing the distinction; I feel an affinity with Ms Malik. I write and have written newspaper columns for several publications over the last forty years (Gosh! Did I have to confess that?) but will never write a blog.

On first reading these pages you may think, gentle reader, that our writer has distinct and firm views and I agree that at times the paragraphs read very much like it; but as you progress through the pages you encounter a mind coming to terms with phenomena and wondering about them. This is a gift and an endearing one.

The cartoons, which accompany the columns, are not intended as caricatures of the characters the writing depicts, but manage to capture the moments and the subtle comedy of each.

Read on!

—Farrukh Dhondy

The Flavour of Love

Along with everything else that Valentine's Day is promoted to be, it is also considered a day of love.

At least that is what the greeting card companies would like us to believe. But here it is not any ordinary love that we are talking about. The emphasis on this particular date, which falls in the month of February, is on romantic love. You know, the kind that Shakespeare made famous in his play, *Love's Labour's Lost*.

The understanding, of course, is for the prospective lovers to find love, and not to lose it. So, how does one discover it? Romantic love, that is. And where exactly does one go looking for this elusive thing?

Soon after his engagement to Lady Diana, when Prince Charles was asked if he was in love, he said, "of course, whatever love means". This ambivalent answer was a sort of precursor to their unhappy marriage. It left his future bride, as well as countless psychoanalysts, completely flummoxed.

If you investigate some of the bestselling musical albums worldwide, you will find strange lyrics like *'What's love got to do with it, what's love but a second-hand emotion'* by Tina Turner.

Or, *'What is love, baby don't hurt me, don't hurt me, no more'* by a singer called Haddaway. This number, when released by the artist in 1993, resonated with so many people that it broke all records in global sales.

Does romantic love always hurt?

C.S. Lewis, the acclaimed novelist, poet and academician, said

in his book *The Four Loves*, 'There is no safe investment. To love at all is to be vulnerable. Love anything, and your heart will certainly be wrung and possibly be broken. If you want to make sure of keeping it intact, you must give your heart to no one, not even to an animal. Wrap it carefully round with hobbies and little luxuries, avoid all entanglements, lock it up safe in the casket or coffin of your selfishness'.

Right! In other words, is the entire exercise in loving undertaken only to experience heartbreak? If not, then who are the people that celebrate love? Why does the entire world love a lover? Where are those lucky in love found? What sustains romantic love? How does love conquer all? When to identify that one is in love?

I remember putting my mother through all these queries.

"You will simply know it, when the right man comes along," she would reply in her most placid voice.

"How will I recognise him?" I persisted.

"Any specific signs I should be looking for?" I prodded.

But my subsequent inquisition would be clubbed together, under the same stoic response.

I never got around to analysing love, but this Valentine's Day I cornered my spouse of twenty-five years.

"When did you know I was the right person for you?" I asked him over breakfast.

"Yes dear," he mumbled, from behind a newspaper.

"You are not answering my question," I accused.

"Yes dear," he repeated.

"You never listen to me, why do I even waste my breath," I exclaimed, about to stomp off.

"From the very first moment that I saw you, you were wearing turquoise dungarees, a bright yellow shirt and silver bangles from wrists till elbows. You looked like a gypsy and I wanted to spend the rest of my life with you," he said with twinkling eyes, lowering the paper.

Love, actually?

Cooking Rhapsody

It is no secret in my household that I dislike cooking.
In all fairness, it should have been a major preoccupation of
mine, considering I spend every waking and sleeping moment with
foodies. But alas! It's just one of those things that refused to take a
hold on me.

My family is obsessed with food. Every key discussion,
argument and quarrel involves some aspect of cooking or eating.
All celebrations, revelry, and festivities include the planning,
provision and eating of food, so very often the wars of the
comestibles break out. They are sometimes resolved by outright
victory for one or other combatant, but mostly through peace treaties
involving reluctant reconciliation.

Even while having one meal, we have been known to get into
a squabble over the next one. It is difficult for strangers, if they
ever overhear our conversation, to make head or tail of it. Mostly,
it does not make sense to us, either.

Why is it that we cannot enjoy one feast before planning a
subsequent one? We can, and we should. But meticulous detail about
a future dish makes its presence felt. And we go right back to
bickering.

The moodiness of the domestic staff that I have hired over the
years has ensured that I do not completely lose touch with matters
pertaining to cooking. More often than not, the maids are indisposed,
and I find myself tying the apron strings around my own ample
waist.

Hence, I know all the intricacies associated with an individual cuisine. Which particular herb spices up a bland offering, and what to add to reduce the sharpness of an extra hot curry, I have it all down to a 't'.

But it is a good idea to stay away from me when I am wielding a kitchen knife. There is no telling exactly what, or even who, might land up on the chopping board. Till the dish does not resemble a mental picture I have of the final product, I am like a woman possessed.

My spouse is mistakenly influenced by the television shows where, in a culinary demonstration, the chefs smile serenely at the camera. He thinks cooking is as easy as a walk in the park, and cannot understand why I make such a fuss over something so trivial.

That is why, last week, the moment our cook called in sick, he offered to rustle up dinner. I was horrified at the suggestion because in over two decades of married life, I had never seen him even boil an egg.

"You don't have to do a thing; just show me where everything in the kitchen is, that's all," my husband assured me.

"Okay," I mumbled, reluctantly.

"Two onions, three tomatoes, ginger and garlic," he announced.

"And coriander leaves," I reminded him.

"Can you please grind them while I cut up the cheese?" he instructed.

"Finished, can I go now?" I asked, a moment or two later.

"Fry it till golden brown, will you?" he requested.

"I thought you were cooking," I complained.

"I am slicing the cheese, see," he said, without lifting his head.

"I think it's done," I muttered, ready to escape.

"Just add the salt, pepper and the rest of the garnishing too," he ordered.

"But you?" I began.

"Are chopping the cheese!" we said in unison.

Oh, well!

Mother Special

I must confess that I was a very reluctant mother.

Motherhood came to me when I was least expecting it. There were so many things I wanted to do before having a child: a glittering career had to be chalked out, books written, places visited, mountains climbed, the list was endless.

But nature intervened, as it usually does, and altered all my plans.

My pregnancy was like a walk in the clouds – it was flawless. I was healthy and cheerful and glowed like sunshine.

A friend of mine, who was also in her first trimester, had terrible morning sickness and doubled up with nausea almost everyday. I had no such problems, and took full advantage of the kindness that people extended towards me.

My belly did not protrude too much initially. To catch the attention of the maître d', and get a good table at a restaurant, I used to exaggeratedly curve my back and pat my stomach. The same ploy meant I was offered seats in crowded buses or trains, and airline stewards happily carried my heavy handbag.

Vegetable sellers started delivering the groceries to my doorstep and elderly ladies would give me suggestions, for free. The world was a joyful place to bring my baby into.

The first thing that happened, as soon as I became a brand new mother, was that I instantly began to empathise with my own

mum. A surge of compassion overcame me, and I felt closer to her than ever before. I looked at her with fresh respect, and whenever I recalled her caring gestures, I could not stop blinking back tears.

She had always been special to me, but after I went through the long labour pangs myself, I developed a gentleness and understanding towards her which was lacking before. I promised myself to be as selfless in my maternal dealings as she was.

I mark the days I remember my mother as my own personal 'Mother's Days'. They could fall on any part of the week or month, but I think of her, and my heart fills with gladness.

I was blessed with a very loving mom. Every mother is extraordinary, and mine was exceptional too.

When I lost her ten years ago, I thought my life would come to an end. I could not function with the idea that I would no longer be able to hear her voice, see her smile or feel her touch.

It was the single most devastating moment of my life. A little bit of me perished with her.

That part is hard to resurrect. I miss her intensely. So do my siblings and her large group of friends. She signified different things to various people.

Her name was Neer, which means water, and like the precious liquid, she was invaluable to all of us.

She was, however, a woman of contradictions.

A wonderful singer, she had a full throated voice and could brighten up any gathering by her sheer presence. She would give musical performances for free in support of charity, but would haggle with a market-vendor over the price of tomatoes.

This May, she would have been seventy-two years old.

It is said that every woman turns into her mother eventually. I can't wait to become mine.

Sibling Rivalry

There is nothing particularly amazing about having siblings. We don't have much of a choice in the matter anyway. Our parents, nature and God are more involved in this evolution process. And before we know it, the stork brings the baby home, and we are introduced to them as brothers or sisters.

Positioning is very important in a family, with the oldest, youngest, and the middle orders being assigned, through tradition, with their own powers and privileges.

My heart goes out to the eldest child in every household. Some of them do not have a childhood of their own. At an age when they themselves need to be babied, they are expected to be responsible for the younger ones. It's an unwritten rule in many families and in certain customs it goes unquestioned.

I have seen two-year-old toddlers getting out of their prams, and offering this mobile form of conveyance to their siblings, or sharing their pacifiers, rattles, toys and even mashed food. Older children assume a natural leadership and get used to being followed by the younger ones.

Some of them carry on in this fashion even when they are adults. They do not realise that their manner is dictatorial, because they have acted like that from a very early age. They also do not understand why their behaviour is construed as overpowering or controlling.

Conversely, youngest children in a brood never really grow up. They get so used to someone watching over them that they find it difficult to think for themselves. Leaving all the decision-making to others, they know that to get out of a sticky situation, all they need to do is call out.

The middle children are a most confused lot. Not happy to lead, nor be able to blindly follow, they carry a sense of maladjustment about themselves. Most of them overcome it in the long run, but some find it difficult to do so.

There is, I believe, empirical evidence to prove that men raised around sisters are more demonstrative, affectionate and fashion-conscious. Also, women raised around brothers are less shy, squeamish or reserved.

Personally, I've been blessed with two siblings. One is older and the other younger. My elder brother was just three when I was born.

My fiercest babyhood battles were fought with him. My dolls would be beheaded and his toy cars crushed. But he went on to become my friend, philosopher and guide. It was he who taught me swimming, fishing, rifle-shooting, riding, singing and using chopsticks.

My younger brother made an unplanned entry into our lives. One evening we had gone to watch a movie with our father while our mother was in the clinic, and the next day she presented us with a baby.

Suddenly, he was the center of everyone's attention.

Six days later I tried to return him to the hospital.

"You can't give him back," my dad exclaimed.

"Why not?" I asked.

"He is your brother. You have to look after him," my father reasoned.

"For how long?" I enquired.

"The rest of your life," he announced.

"He will also break my dolls!" I said, bursting into tears.

"No, he is your real life doll, see?" My father stated, putting him in my lap.

That's how the bond started.

Battle of the Bulge

This morning I woke up feeling overweight.
I knew I had gained weight because even my footsteps sounded heavy.

"Do you think I am fat?" I asked spouse.

"Huh, Huh," he replied vaguely.

"Can you please tell me?" I prodded.

"Do you think you are fat?" he countered.

"Yes," I muttered.

"Ok," he agreed, hurrying out of the room.

"This is serious stuff," said the voice in my head. "Better get cracking, before those fat cells swell to make me double in size."

Pulling my gym gear out of hibernation, I tried to fit into it. The t-shirt had shrunk at the arms and the track pants were biting around my waist. My clothes were contracting at an alarming rate.

Tying my shoelaces into a determined knot, I reached for the car keys. On the way out, I grabbed a handful of dried nuts. I had read somewhere that one must never exercise on an empty stomach. The writer must obviously be fond of eating to make sweeping statements like that. Or perhaps this was indeed a scientific fact. I decided to give it the benefit of doubt while munching on pistachios.

In the fitness center, all eyes were on me. The men and women there looked extremely healthy, and were bursting with energy. I tried to merge with the crowd, but felt like it was my first day at school.

Looking around I realised that most of the people did not need to burn calories. They were trimmed and toned like professional models. Maybe they *were* professional models, hired to increase the glamour quotient of the place, who knows?

Finding a spot on the floor of the aerobics studio, I marked it with my water bottle and positioned myself on the second row: it was neither too close to the instructor, nor very far away. Flexing my limbs, I pretended to be a regular exercise junkie, and got sympathetic smiles from my co-exercisers.

A few minutes before the appointed hour, the trainers walked in. There were two of them, and had perfectly chiseled bodies, as though carved in flexible stone. One fidgeted with the music system, while the other fitted a wired microphone, which curved around his face.

The class started with me in top form. I was totally blinded in my admiration of the two instructors and was slightly smitten by their gorgeous looks as well.

Huffing and puffing I kept up with them, step for agonizing step. Glancing at the big clock on the wall, I realised that it had only been ten minutes and I was already getting out of breath.

Midway through the class I thought I saw a mean streak surface in the trainers as they kept pushing us. My enthusiasm was vanishing faster than the drops of sweat on my forehead.

Towards the end, I saw them in their true light as their nagging voice began to grate on my nerves. The last set was complete torture and if I could lift my foot, I would have happily kicked one, or both, of the wicked bullies.

In the evening, the muscle cramps set in. Every movement brought me misery and I had no option but to sit perfectly still on the easy chair.

"My new jeans don't fit me, Mom, do you think I am fat?" asked my skinny daughter.

"Huh, Huh," I replied, with my eyes closed.

Silent Treatment

We, the female of the species, are made to carry a lot of unwanted baggage.

From time immemorial, we have been tagged with various labels that are totally ambiguous. Like: beautiful but dumb, bright but unattractive, effusive but arrogant, knowledgeable but conceited.

In our formative years, these harsh generalizations bother us somewhat, but with time we outgrow them. We learn to have faith in our own judgement, gain confidence in ourselves, and begin to view the unnecessary labelling with amusement.

But what is more difficult to come to terms with is our collective inability to get over the sulk.

What is that you ask? Well, in simple words, it is a phrase used to describe a bad mood. When we are morose, glum, displeased, gloomy, upset or plain depressed, we sulk.

Sulk, like the definition of the English verb, is a doing word.

Yet, contrary to what it suggests, while sulking one does nothing, least of all, talk. This silent treatment is the greatest weapon in a woman's armoury. Our manly counterparts can outsmart us in many aspects, but when we go on a non-talking mode, the war is won even without going into battle. Well, usually.

Sulking, incidentally, is quite different from throwing a tantrum.

The latter terminology involves a vociferous demand for something, and is accompanied by an outburst of temper and a stamping of feet. This is typical childish behaviour, which sometimes follows us into adulthood, but is not accepted very well, sociologically. However, going on a sulk is a universal phenomenon, at least in the entire of womankind.

So, what is it exactly that makes us sulk and give up speaking, albeit temporarily?

Talking is one of the most enjoyable activities that we indulge in, and is the very essence of our existence. Why do we place a halt on it? Who is responsible for putting us in this state? And the most important question of all, how do the non-sulky men in our lives, handle us constantly sulky ones?

To answer the last one first, the best way is to leave us alone whenever we are enveloped in such a disposition. Excessive prodding leads to the sulking period getting extended. But, there is a sort of fine balance here. If you abandon us for too long in our own company, the result is not good either. The length of the silent treatment could again increase.

Equilibrium has to be maintained individually, as the case may be, by each set of sparring partners.

Why do we sulk? Now that depends on a wide range of issues, from the minuscule to the absolute. Some of us sulk at the drop of a hat, at real or imagined rebuffs. Others are more accommodating, and only resort to sulking to cool an argument.

But one thing that life teaches is this: nothing scares a man more than a woman going silent on him.

Last night, when we took the fifth wrong turn at a precarious roundabout in peak traffic, I just gave up. My husband would not take directions from me, so I reclined back into the passenger seat and closed my eyes. Determinedly, I chose to respond with complete silence to his next several queries.

"Why are you not saying anything?" spouse asked worriedly.

I continued to keep mum.

"See you were right, I'm taking the turn you suggested," he conceded.

Slowly and silently the treatment always works!

Not a Cloud in the Sky

A few years back, if I were asked to describe myself as an optimist or pessimist, I would say I was very hopeful and forward looking.

I did have an annoying tendency to expect the best possible outcome, and dwell on the brighter side of things.

Or perhaps it was just the habit of exaggeration. For instance, whenever I saw a glass, even a quarter full, I might refer to it as overflowing. If I went for a job interview, I started promising dinner treats in anticipation of success and when I heard a bird singing, I would declare that this was paradise.

The peculiar thing was, or is, that no one inspired me to think like this. It just came naturally to me. In my clumsy fashion, I assumed that it was how the rest of mankind perceived the universe to be as well. You know, full of sugar and spice and everything nice.

Friends warned me against viewing the world through permanent rose filtered glasses, but I persevered.

People were nice to me, oh so nice.

Once, I was late for a movie, and the usher explained the bit I had missed, while escorting me to my seat. In another instance, I got lost finding a restaurant in downtown Toronto, and the cabbie, seeing the place had closed for the night, not only waived the fare, but also invited my family for dinner at his own house.

One more time, I dropped an expensive bracelet in a crowded

restaurant. I walked back to the cafe, confident that I would find it there. Sure enough, the owner handed it back saying he had looked after it for me.

These incidences just reiterated my belief that there was genuine goodness in people. And if there were two sides to every coin, the one facing me was on a permanent, sunny side up.

But life is a great leveller and personal grief taught me that everything was not hunky-dory. Coming to terms with the demise of loved ones swung me into severe misery. For a period of time, the world looked bleak, and I could not cope with my intense grief.

In this unhappy state, I started observing everything with hopelessness. If I was caught in a traffic jam on the way to the airport, I was sure I would miss the flight. When the telephone rang in the middle of the night, I assumed it brought terrible news, and if a stranger tried speaking to me, I thought I was on my way to getting fleeced.

Things turned from bad to worse when I started avoiding people with a cheerful disposition. Their jolly gusto and happy laughter irritated me.

Most reluctantly, I decided to get a hold on myself, grit my teeth and put up with the next enthusiastically jovial person.

"What a bright sunny day!" My spouse announced in order to get me out of my blues.

"Yeah!" I grunted in response.

"Not a cloud in the sky," he continued.

"What will you do if I point them out?" I challenged.

"I will give you a dollar per cloud," he smiled.

"Now you're talking," I muttered to myself.

Driving from the house to the center of town, I was richer by twenty bucks. By the end of the day, I had amassed a small fortune in the shortest possible time.

For spotting clouds in the sky, should I return to clear-eyed optimism?

Faux Pas

No sooner had I understood the dictionary meaning of faux pas, I got busy making them.

I mean how much more socially outrageous can I be? You will be surprised because I shock even myself. My tongue runs away with my mouth and I become incapable of retrieving it, so thankfully, I shut up. That is the good part.

Sometimes I forget to do so, and more bizarre statements issue forth. Then, short of putting a hand around my throat, to choke myself, I have no other easy way out. And that is the bad part.

I would like to say that it was not always the case. However, age and maturity compel me to admit that, unfortunately, I've always been unpredictable. Time and again, I keep repeating the same mistakes, and learning the same lessons.

On my first ever visit to Amman, Jordan, a city in which I have subsequently lived, I decided to lunch at a roadside open-air cafe. After ordering a regular salad, I saw the waiter still hovering around us. He kept waving the beverage menu in my face.

"Which fruit juices do you have?" I asked impatiently.

"Passion," replied the guy, sotto voce.

"Sorry?" my husband and I chorused together.

"Passion," he repeated in the same monotone.

"Is it fresh passion or bottled?" my spouse asked, smiling broadly.

I tried to kick him under the table but hit the chair leg instead, wincing in agony.

"Fresh passion, Madam. We serve it chilled," he explained, looking at me without blinking.

"Hey Mom, he's flirting with you," our daughter hissed, in a stage whisper.

My kick below the table found its target this time, as she grimaced in pain.

"So, you want to try it?" the waiter asked.

Under the amused gaze of spouse and daughter, I felt a blush rise on my face. Out of sheer curiosity, we asked for a double serving and when the orange-coloured glasses arrived, we realised it was passion-fruit juice, which was simply called '*passion*' all over Amman. Another local custom to be remembered, we reminded each other. No more faux pas, hopefully.

In the airport on the way back, I automatically headed for the executive lounge.

"You are travelling economy lady. This is for upper class passengers only," the gentleman at the entrance told me frostily.

"But my ticket is business class," I said, and then realised that the person at the check-in counter had mistakenly put me in the wrong section.

Trudging downstairs, back through immigration, I was bristling to pick a fight with anyone who stopped me. No one did. I felt cheated somehow. I mean, all that wasted anger.

I marched back with a fresh boarding card, and tried to sail into the lounge this time, almost tripping on the carpet by the door.

"What would you like to drink Ma'am?" the guy serving me was all courtesy now.

"We have coffee, tea, cocktails, passion," he read from the menu.

"Fruit juices are fresh or canned?" I asked.

"Fresh passion Ma'am. We serve it chilled," he smiled.

Oops, I did it again. I should be used to it by now. I will be used to it soon. Next time, watch me, next time.

Dancing Queen

Dancing comes naturally to some people.

It seems to me that the cliché or stereotype of the naturally rhythmic Africans and South Americans is substantially true. It appears in-born. Even when they sway gently to a musical beat, they do so rhythmically.

The several hoards of Brazilians, boogying on the streets of their various cities during football matches, are a case in point. It does not matter whether they are young, old, male, female, sober or inebriated. As soon as a tune is played, they just get up from whatever position they are sitting in, and start to dance. Their movements are so graceful that it is a joy to be even a spectator.

Every country, however, has its own unique kind of dances. Some belong to the classical oeuvre, while others are folksy. The traditional dances take years of training to perfect, and their dancers devote entire lives to achieving this.

The individual dance is a performance, while those involving a partner is a metaphor – for love or the enactment of some drama. Group dances are presentations too, but are often as in Scotland and even with the ludicrous Morris dancing of England, symbolic of some national custom or pride.

My home country India has a great assortment of colourful dances, from the conventional to the modern.

Indian dances vary according to the region they originate from. The orthodox traditional ones represent a particular culture and their steps are based around a strict style. They also make use of *Natya* or acting, to signify mythological or folklore stories.

Births, marriages and religious festivals each have their proper expression in specific dances.

But most of the world recognises us by our Bollywood dances.

The Indian film industry makes movies that are musicals, with lavish song and dance routines. People, who are unfamiliar with India and have only seen it portrayed in cinema, think every Indian, dressed in garish, over the top clothes and jewels, keeps singing all the time.

Try as I might to ignore it, the minute my nationality is discovered in an alien land, I am expected to demonstrate a few steps of any song that a foreigner might remember. From one of our countless films, that is.

Belly dancing, a type of Oriental dance that involves vigorous torso movements, always fascinated me. Everything about this particular dance form is captivating, from the sensual costume to the stimulating steps. Contrary to its name, the emphasis during this dance is not so much on the abdomen, as it is on the hips. Correct posture and muscle control are absolutely essential to perform the intricate moves.

Last week, I gave in to my curiosity and attended a belly-dancing class. The instructor was a stunning looking Jordanian woman who was effortlessly demonstrating the complicated steps.

"Yallah! Move your hips in a figure eight loop," she scolded.

"I'm sorry. I am from India," I blurted out when I could not get the step.

"Al Hind? Like Katrina Kaif?" she exclaimed.

"Yes, she is a top Indian actress," I agreed.

"You know the *Mashallah* song?" she asked, wriggling her back.

"No," I lied.

"Why not? Come to the front of the class and give a demonstration," she ordered.

"Mashallah Mashallah," I flapped my arms and danced.

Teaching the teacher?

In Sickness and in Health

I was waiting to fall sick for a long time.

I did not wish for a sinister kind of illness to befall me. No, I was happy to have some sort of a gentle discomfort to wrestle with. You know, the type where one is mildly incapacitated.

Why was I making this bizarre aspiration? No great reason, other than that fact that I wanted to document the misfortune. And do it most objectively, with me being the subject of the study. I mean, given a chance between wishing ill of someone else, or turning the tables on myself, I chose the latter.

Where wishes go, this was somewhat peculiar, I admit, and I do warn all readers against following my example. But in order to do justice to the research, I decided to become my own proverbial guinea pig.

Unlike the poor animals used in laboratory experiments that are induced with a particular bug forcefully, I waited for Mother Nature to do the trick. Not partial to faulty cravings, she also took her time.

People were falling sick around me: left, right and centre. But I was positioned, as if inside a protective cocoon, and managed to evade the germs, every time. The result was that I did not suffer, but my pending investigation work did. The deadlines would be made, broken, remade, and I was still in the pink of health.

When plans were drawn up to visit my home country during the summer, I had a moment of reassurance. Time to roll up those sleeves, I said to myself. Not long to wait now. There was no way I could survive the rainy season in India without falling ill. It was almost a given.

But a fortnight into my three-week vacation, despite the flooded airport tarmacs and congested roadblocks, I was fighting fit. This was not going according to plan.

"The holiday is almost over and I have not even fallen sick," I complained to my spouse a day before leaving my homeland.

Rat-a-tat-a-tat was the sound I heard in response.

Turning back I saw him rapping a wooden headboard of the bed, quite forcefully, with his knuckles. "He has become dreadfully superstitious," said the voice in my head.

Next morning I woke up with a giant sneeze. Ten minutes later, I got a paroxysm of coughing so bad that I felt the shaking of the ground beneath my feet. My forehead was on fire, and I had difficulty swallowing anything.

In all this pandemonium, all I wanted was to get quickly to my laptop, and meticulously begin documenting my much-coveted illness.

"What are you doing? Why are you grinning? My God! You are burning with fever," my husband exclaimed.

"I want to write the diary of a sick woman as authentically as possible. Can you pass my iPad please," I croaked.

"You wished this upon yourself? Are you crazy?" he said.

What followed was a lecture too colourful to recount and it interfered with the filing of my report. But I persevered.

Twisting and turning in delirium, I kept the account accurate. The fever broke on the sixth day.

Weak with relief, I made the following page entry: never overestimate the power of knocking wood.

Rat-a-tat-a-tat.

Brows Right

It might not be common knowledge, but women lose a lot of sleep over their eyebrows.

The arch of hair, above each eye-socket, by virtue of its thickness or thinness, generates an unreasonable amount of anxiety in us. Numerous face-reading experts have made fortunes out of this uneasiness, exploiting it to the hilt.

Eye-shaping parlours also do brisk business by claiming to enhance your looks by tweaking a hair here, or patting one there.

Where eyebrows are concerned, there are only two things that can trouble you: having too much hair, or alternately, too little of it. There is not much one can do about this, as certain ethnicities veer towards bushy eyebrows, while others are plagued by near invisible ones.

In Amman, the problem is of the former variety. Thick, unruly and shaggy brows are a norm and everyone is caught in a quest to tame them. Waxing, threading and tweezing services are generously offered in any hairdressing salon, irrespective of whether you are a male or female.

There is hardly any social awkwardness associated with it. On the contrary, frank and candid opinions are exchanged, over how assistance can be provided in shaping them into some semblance of normalcy.

When I was new to the country, I would wonder why I was constantly getting mistaken for a Jordanian. By almost everybody I came into contact with, that is. It was disclosed to me one day by,

of all people, a four-year-old boy. He kept toddling up to my table and, instead of my mouth, he would wave a half-eaten cookie at my forehead.

The mother, who was extremely apologetic, explained while bundling him off, that I resembled one of her relatives so much that I could pass off for her twin.

"She has the same bushy eyebrows like yours," she said. "Why don't you go to golden touch?" she added helpfully.

It took me some time to figure out what she meant. *Golden Touch*, it turned out, was the name of a local beauty parlour that specialised in shaping the brow. On further investigation, I was told that it had closed down, but another one had opened nearby, and was doing brisk business.

Very soon I found myself walking through some freshly painted doors into the plush interiors of a brand new salon. Two of its walls were coloured maroon to match the cushioned chairs, which were placed in front of illuminated mirrors.

I was invited to sit, and then handed a menu card. It ran into several pages, which had details on each and every type of eyebrow grooming one could ever think of.

I was mesmerised.

'A locked eyebrow is a sign of a sad person. You can never know what to expect from them. Straight eyebrows suggest melancholic nature, and short ones symbolise a weak intellect,' I read from the folder.

'Long eyebrows connote a sharp brain, but such people are also unpredictable and volatile. Thick, dark and abundant brows hint at a dominant and willful personality in a man. But on a woman, it represents a flirtatious nature. They are fun loving and laugh a lot,' I learned.

Before anyone could notice my absence, I got up and beat a hasty retreat.

If what I read was true, and indeed I was born to laughingly flirt, why raise an eyebrow about it?

Photo Agony

The advent of cell-phones has done away with the need for carrying a camera.

These devices, depending on their pixels, generate a picture with varying degrees of clarity. The result is that all mobile phone users can shoot any scene, face or event that catches their fancy, and store it for posterity.

This is not necessarily a bad thing, but the result is that it has taken away the charm of still photography. In the days gone by, a photographer was a much-cherished invitee, at any family gathering of importance.

They would be quite unlike the gentlemen who appear nowadays in some formal functions. The current breed has a disinterested attitude, because they know that the pictures they click will not be the most appealing ones. Some casual onlooker could, with a swish of his phone camera, produce more eye-catching photos.

But the earlier photographers had no such insecurities to worry about. Hence, they had a sense of purpose about them. They did not believe in taking haphazard shots. There was method and planning involved in creating every masterpiece.

Balance, symmetry and background had to be taken into consideration, even before the subjects were asked to pose.

It is said that a camera never lies, and that a picture is worth a thousand words. But one thing I can tell you is that the cameras that these erstwhile photographers used were big time liars.

Maybe it had to do with the shine of the film in which the photo was printed, or the angle of the chin that the photographer tilted, but the end product would be a photograph that was so luminous that it had scant resemblance to the original subject. Whether it was a portrait shot of a lady or a child, they all looked alluringly beautiful. Even the portraiture of gentlemen had an underlying glossiness about it.

Recently, after being turned away from two embassies for having the wrong specifications for a visa photo, I had to go to a studio, all over again.

The photographer was from my grandfather's generation and had an old-world charm about him. He greeted me courteously and, despite my protests, offered me Turkish coffee in a small cup.

After making small talk, he asked me if I wanted to powder my nose. Noticing a large mirror with combs, brushes and make-up stuff in front of it, I shook my head in the negative.

"You can go through this way, carry on," he insisted, pointing towards the toilet.

I had no choice but to use the washroom.

"I will take twelve pictures, six non-smiling ones for your visa, and the rest for your collection. I am an artist you see," he told me firmly.

For the next thirty minutes, I was in pure agony as he fussed over every angle of my face.

"Just grin and bear it," said the voice in my head.

After some more cups of Turkish coffee, he produced the photos for my inspection. One glance at them and I was struck dumb.

They lied of course, but if truth is told, I looked no less than a film star in those magical shots.

"Was it worth the wait? What do you think?" asked the veteran photographer.

"Picture perfect," I replied.

Pen Friends

There was an age when people wrote lengthy and loving letters, which were addressed to family, friends or inamoratas.

They came in sealed envelopes and you needed a paper knife to unseal them.

These were personal letters of course, written in long hand, some in beautiful cursive and others in an unintelligible scrawl. There were stamps attached on the cover, which announced the place from where the missive had travelled. If one looked carefully, there would be the mark of a post office seal on it too.

Writing letters was quite a time-consuming job. Jane Austen's characters spent a large part of their day involved in this activity. She was a great woman of letters as well.

'I have now attained the true art of letter-writing, which we are always told, is to express on paper exactly what one would say to the same person by word of mouth,' Jane Austen wrote in *My dear Cassandra*, a compilation of letters to her sister.

Polishing the skill of correspondence was an integral job of a teacher at school. There was a designated method to it, as in learning the various forms of address, the terms of greeting that were acceptable, the precise manner to inquire about the receiver's health, where to put the comma after the endearment and, most importantly, how to conclude the letter.

If one forgot something, there was a concession in the way of a *P.S.* that would allow the writer to scribble the earlier overlooked

thought. Nobody remembered what the abbreviated letters stood for, or what *R.S.V.P.* in an invite actually meant, but it generally enhanced the business of correspondence.

Plus, there were the professional letter writers. In the villages of my home country, the illiterate folk would pay them in cash or kind, for their efforts. Occasionally, it boiled down to the postman's responsibility who along with delivering the letters, would be coaxed into reading them aloud, and writing the responses too.

Personally, ever since I mastered the trick of stringing together words on paper, I have been writing letters.

But, I was rather unlucky in my choice of pen friends. When I was younger, I wrote letters to people who never replied to me. Like: Santa Claus, God, the Tooth Fairy, Cinderella, and even Enid Blyton. I would pour my heart out to them, but it was an exercise in futility.

In senior school, I had met a girl called Tanya. She was visiting my town for a few days, before going back to Moscow. She decided to write to me regularly and I was delighted.

But unfortunately all her letters were in Russian, and other than admiring the doodle-like words, I could not decipher much of it. After such a tragedy, I decided to steer clear of friendship by post.

However, to my complete surprise, quite recently, nature handed me a pen friend on a platter, one more time. And as if to make up for lost time, two arrived at once.

In this age of the electronic mail, one cannot use the term 'pen pal' in its traditional sense any longer, but you know what I mean.

Expressive, informative and descriptive letters make their way to me, from lives that are alien to mine, and I am over the moon.

As a postscript, I am thinking of writing a 'thank you' note to dear God in heaven, once again.

He might respond, who knows?

Darling Ladies

If you train your eyes to it, you can easily spot these women in any social gathering.

They are all of a certain age, well maintained and elegantly turned out. With their impeccable mannerisms, they usually attract a small group of followers, who hover around them.

Listening to their talk, you realise that these vivacious women have another thing in common: they address everybody by an identical moniker. They call everyone darling.

The endearment of choice is always the same; there is no mistaking that. It never deviates to sweetheart, beloved, or even the saccharine sounding, sweetie. They stick to the original format, and do not make any changes in their manner of speaking.

I never really liked these darling ladies. There was something about them, which I found unappealing. It troubled me that they could not identify people by their given name, but clubbed all and sundry together with one universally common nomenclature.

I considered them as plain lazy, or dumb, sometimes both. I wondered why they could not make a little extra effort to remember individuals. In fact, not just family, friends or acquaintances, but I saw them call out to their pets also, in a similar manner.

But the strange thing was that this affected nobody, not a single person, other than me. Let alone get annoyed, everyone they interacted with seemed to relish the attention.

The lap dogs perked up their ears and came bounding to the

mistresses, the cats purred in response, and the rabbits hopped in joy. The dry cleaner took extra care with the clothes, the photograph assistant photoshopped every picture, the young lady artist gave an extra two percent discount on her paintings and so on.

And, all because they were called: *darling*.

How do I know this? I trailed a glamorous aunt of mine for one day and saw her work the magic word. She used it frequently and generously. Her frail form would light up every time she got a positive response from the people she so addressed.

The folks she spoke to would be transformed too. They engaged her in warmth and went out of their way to please her. It was a delight to behold.

Tentatively and very apprehensively I decided to try it out for myself. First I had to train myself to discard my earlier biases. But as time went by, it became easier, because I was suddenly forgetting names. Maybe it had to do with my advancing years, but I did not want to dwell too much on this rather mundane aspect of my life

So, when I blanked out one more time, while talking to a person I was recently introduced to, I just filled the awkward pause with: *darling*.

The reaction I got was absolutely unbelievable. The dour faced man became friendliness personified. He smiled, held the door open, escorted me to my car, and even wished me a polite goodbye.

Since then I have been on a roll. From obtaining the best cinema seats and restaurant table reservations to getting the fastest haircuts and pedicure services, I have secured them all, simply by using this favoured word.

It still does not roll off my tongue as naturally as it should be, but I am getting there.

Ah yes, and I am now, a darling lady!

The Head that Aches

God forbid, but if one must wish ill of someone, from the entire list of misfortunes that can be unhappily coveted, the pain in the head should be the last.

Why any sane person would desire a calamity to befall another individual is a matter of philosophical discussion. This can be debated on a different platform.

Be that as it may, a headache is something that even one's worst enemies should not be asked to suffer, especially if it is of the migraine variety.

Every ache and pain is difficult to tolerate, but one somehow gets habituated to it. However, migraine headaches are things one can never really get used to. These debilitating attacks are like blows to the head that creep upon the sufferer without notice, and leave you reeling in its aftermath.

Incidentally, researching this leads to disappointment because headache is actually termed as a *'non-specific symptom'* which means that it is something that is subjective, and noticed by the patient, but cannot be measured directly, like say, your blood pressure. It does not portend any specific disease, and because it is self-reported, it is not taken very seriously.

In fact, the only thing good about migraine is its exotic sounding name. Derived from the Greek word *hemikrania*, it is perfectly described as: *'pain on one side of the head'*. The good news, however, begins and ends there.

A normal outbreak of this ailment can last from two to seventy-two hours, and leaves the patient weak-kneeded and hollow bodied.

I have first-hand knowledge of the disorder. Having endured its worst attacks where, if I were handed an axe, I would have willingly chopped off my own head, I live to tell the tale.

Since there is no cure for it, over the years I have taught myself to manage the pain. I try and avoid all its triggers, like bright sunlight, smoky rooms, emotional disturbances, and so on. The result is that the frequency, intensity and duration of the episodes have decreased.

But once in a while they recur.

The other day I was reclining on a tilted chair in the midst of a terrible migraine spell, when my cell phone beeped a message. My concerned friends were sending in frantic suggestions.

"Rub Tiger Balm on your eyelids. It will hurt like crazy but once the sting subsides, so will the pain," I read through a blurry haze.

In sheer desperation, I reached for the bottle of the pungent ointment, and smeared generous amounts of it on the lids of my eyes.

The next instant I almost passed out. The intense burning sensation clashed with the hammer-like knocks on my head. My eyes felt like they were being gouged out.

"You deserve to die for listening to loony ideas," said the voice in my head.

But twenty minutes later, unexpectedly, my skull turned numb and the pain vanished. Just like that. I could hardly believe my smarting eyes.

Since then, I carry a small bottle in my handbag at all times, and dole it out magnanimously to all headache sufferers.

And what do I call the magic treatment? Eye of the Tiger, of course!

House Hen

There are a few rules that I have made in my home. I try to apply them to my family and myself as diligently as possible. For instance: no consumption of meals in front of the television; no talking to the hired help in a disrespectful manner; switching off the lights when stepping out of a room; eating up all the food that is dished out, and so on and so forth.

These guidelines are easily understood and adhered to by all of us.

Certain hours of the week I have earmarked as my compulsory workdays. It helps me in disciplining myself, and meeting my deadlines. But the problem arises during weekends when the rest of the world relaxes, with schools, offices, factories and shops closed, while I am left to slave away at my computer, because in my own little universe, it is a time for toil.

In order to take my work seriously, the most important regulation I have drafted is that under no circumstance should I be disturbed when I am locked up in the study.

To emphasise the point, I told my domestic workers I should not be disturbed for petty disasters – only the ones as serious as a sudden accident, an unexpected fire or a drastic earthquake. While I was working, that is.

A few clarifications of this were needed for my over enthusiastic staff. Does the collapse of a garden shed qualify? Or, is running out of cooking gas a disaster or not? Having sorted this out, I am, in general, left alone.

But there is an old proverb in my mother tongue Hindi, which roughly translated states that *house-hens and home grown lentils have the same value.* It means that even the most successful individuals, are taken for granted within the four walls of their household.

I should know, I am a case in point. Nobody takes my job seriously in my family. And since I don't dress myself in a formal jacket, or move around with an important briefcase bulging with official documents, my occupation is not considered significant.

As a writer, my work clothes consist of sweat pants, and oversized faded t-shirts. This is too casual a look to be associated with any sense of authority. Or sobriety.

Also magically, my cellphone, which sometimes does not ring for so long that I even forget what my ringtone sounds like, starts ringing the minute I step into my den.

Why can't I put it on silent? Of course I should, but the worry that someone might die in far off lands, while my phone is on a quiet mode, prevents me from doing that.

But this morning my writing was cruising along smoothly, when I heard some commotion outside my door.

"Why are you here today?" my housemaid hissed.

"Water pressure-pump problem." That sounded like the plumber.

"Hush! Not so loud. Who called you?" she asked in a stage whisper.

"Why are you shrieking?" he asked.

"Shhhh! Come tomorrow," she said.

"You shhhh yourself, and call Madam," he snapped.

"Is the house on fire? You had an accident? Earthquake coming?" she ticked off the memorised list.

"No, no and no," he answered.

"Then go, go and go," she dismissed him.

"I must raise her salary," said the voice in my head!

Caught Napping

Sleep, I must admit, is a wonderful state of being.
As Shakespeare said it's the '*chief nourisher in life's feast,*'
While we are sleeping, our bodies are rejuvenated. We wake up from our slumbers, restored and energised, to face a new day with all its challenges.

Unlike walking and talking, no one has to really teach us how to sleep. Babies sleep round the clock and have little concept of day or night. Their enthusiastic mothers have to, rather, train them to stay awake. This they do by trial and error. Sometimes they fall into an exhausted doze while their energetic offspring continue to gurgle in delight. But here I digress.

Research shows that folks who face sleep deprivation suffer a number of health issues including irregular heartbeat, high blood pressure, diabetes and so on.

It can also make you forgetful, depressive and obese. As if all this is not bad enough, it also leads to, what one survey describes very delicately, marital strife. It did not clarify the last bit, so I am not going to explain what that might mean.

According to Shakespeare, Julius Caesar preferred the company of folks '*that are fat, sleek-headed men and such as sleep a-nights. Yon Cassius hath a lean and hungry look. He thinks too much; such men are dangerous.*'

In Macbeth, he equates the murder of the sleeping king with

the murder of sleep itself. '*Sleep no more for Macbeth doth murder Sleep*....'

The general rule is that everyone dozes at night, once the moon comes out and dinner is over. But in some societies, there is a concept of an afternoon nap too.

The 'siesta' is a snooze-time that follows lunch break. Followed in hot countries, where the sun is at its scorching best during high noon, people drop off to sleep for a short period of time, right after their mid-day meal.

In these cultures, their day is divided into three parts. The pre-nap morning chunk: where most of the physically challenging tasks are completed.

The intermediary naptime: here everything comes to a standstill, and the entire town, sort of, drops dead.

And the post nap: lethargic pen pushing sluggishness that is followed by hectic socialising.

If you ask me, I think only physically ill people need to be found in bed during daytime. Even when I am sick, I prefer to sit up in a chair, rather than stretch on a cot, before sundown.

But recently, I was terribly jet-lagged after coming back from a trip to the United States. My body was trying to adjust to the difference in the time zones. At twelve in the afternoon, my head touched a pillow and before I could stop myself, I passed into oblivion.

"What are you doing?" I heard a faint voice.

"Counting till hundred," I mumbled automatically.

"With eyes closed?" the accusation continued.

"They are semi-open," I lied.

"In four hours how far have you reached?" the voice asked.

"I've been sleeping for so long?" I sat up with a jump.

"Caught napping!" my husband grinned, and ducked as a cushion went sailing over his head.

Meditation Diary

Saturday: I wake up with a severe headache.
The sound of an advertising jingle is reverberating in my ears. I realise that I had gone to sleep listening to the news on television.

"I'm going to start meditating from today," I inform my husband.

He is busy answering emails on his Blackberry, and ignores me completely.

I spread my yoga mat near a full length French window, and sit down cross-legged.

"What are you doing?" my spouse is aghast.

I get into the lotus position and close my eyes, ignoring him totally.

I tell my brain to blank itself of all thoughts, but a million of them gush into my mind.

Groceries have to be bought, the carpenter has to be called, the stain on my new dress has to be tackled and so on and so forth. After a few more minutes of mental torture, I stretch out my legs, and give up.

Sunday: I decide to first investigate everything I can on meditation and then meditate.

I mean there is no use trying to do something if you are clueless about it, is there?

Monday: I read up all I can about the various forms of meditation. I am more confused now than ever before because I do not know which one to follow.

Abandoning the whole exercise I go for coffee to Starbucks. While there, I help myself to some cheesecake too. My will power has gone for a toss.

Tuesday: Procrastination is getting the better of me. I make a list of errands that I have to run, before I sit down to explore meditation seriously.

The mind has to be totally uncluttered but I don't know how to calm my overactive brain. I cannot concentrate with so many tasks waiting to be completed. And meditation cannot be done in a hurry, or so says the manual.

Wednesday: Determined to learn all I can about the joys of meditating, I start researching early on in the day.

While exploring, I come across a Bruce Lee saying, 'Empty your mind and be formless and shapeless like water.'

'When you put water into a cup, it becomes the cup, you put it into a bottle, it becomes the bottle, you put it in a teapot and it becomes the teapot. Water can flow and change shape. Be water, my friend,' he instructed.

Thursday: Today I decide in quiet desperation, to become water.

I sit cross-legged, close my eyes and try to make my mind vacant. I emphasise on my breath, by counting the movement of air in and out of my lungs.

The exercise lasts barely for five minutes, but I feel a sense of calmness within me.

Friday: I think I have grasped the technique. Except, it is difficult to find the time to follow it.

Later in the day, I find myself sitting in a large auditorium that is facing a stage. On the microphone is a man who is droning on and on about something financial.

I decide to meditate with my eyes open. Within seconds, my mind is clear of all thoughts as I focus on my breathing.

On the seven hundredth breath, I hear loud clapping.

The speech is over, but I have discovered a new way to get through boring evenings.

Cat Chronicles

I have this theory, three theories actually.

The first one is that waiters as a tribe are intuitively trained to walk past your table in a restaurant without making any eye contact with the diners.

The second is that when they do materialise, they mechanically keep filling your water glass, even when you specifically ask them not to.

And the third is that they spit in your food. If you irritate them too much, that is.

The first two I have repeatedly observed and consider to be accurate, and the third I have yet to verify. But my undercover spies are scouting around all the eating joints in the neighbourhood, and they will validate my beliefs very soon.

In the part of town that I live in, cats surround me. Two months back, when I moved here as a brand new resident, the deluge of the feral kitties came as a bolt from the blue. The feline of the species far outnumber any other animal in this place.

There are black cats, white cats, thin cats, fat cats, spotted cats, striped cats, tiny malnourished cats, obese cats, and the rest of the cats of every variation, right here on my doorstep.

One morning I opened the front door to a loud kitty snarl. A rude cat was sleeping on the doormat, and objected to my presence in my own the doorway. It hissed at me before slinking under the nearest potted plant, and continued the catnap.

In this world there are people who love cats and then there are the rest of us. We love dogs, rabbits, turtles, goldfish, canaries, hamsters, parrots, and other kind of domestic pets, but we are terrified of cats.

Maybe it has something to do with all the negative superstitions about these feline creatures in many societies. Like the common belief that a black cat crossing your path leads to bad luck. Or, that they are actually wicked witches in disguise.

It is said that this conviction of cats being witches led to their widespread extermination in Europe during medieval times. But killing them intensified the epidemic of black plague in places where there were not enough cats to keep the rat population down.

The notorious Pied Piper of Hamelin was a *'rat catcher'* initially but when the townsmen went back on their promise, and refused to pay him, he lured away the children of Hamelin and made them disappear.

That is a legendry tale that has survived for eight centuries. But cats are supposed to have nine lives, and killing a cat brings seventeen years of bad luck.

Thus, one must not even think about it. Not that I was thinking along those murderous lines, anyway.

But one day, a mysterious notification arrived in my letter box. It was printed on official looking paper, with an Arabic translation on its reverse side.

In polite but formal tones, it stated that we were hereby notified to keep all our domestic cats indoors, or they would be confiscated and taken away.

I could hardly believe my luck. The cat menace was about to vanish!

It is one month since the optimistic caveat was delivered. Nothing much has happened after the warning missive.

I am still waiting, and the curiosity is killing me.

Who will bell the cat?

Dental Pause

A few decades ago, dentists were not taken seriously. Nobody needed to look for one even in an emergency because there would be many volunteers to help pull out an ailing tooth. I am often told, by people of my parents' generation, for example, about a particular string and door method, which worked perfectly.

The technique was simple. The wayward molar would have a strong thread tied around it. Securely. The other end of it was knotted, to a sturdy door handle.

The patient was placed on a chair, with the mouth open, of course.

Without warning, the door was snapped shut. The suddenness of the action made the painful tooth go flying out of the surprised oral cavity, even before the patient's brain could register the agony.

It was as simple as that.

Barbers, earwax-removers, moustache and beard trimmers, cooks, head massagers, and tailors all doubled up as dentists. In other words, anyone willing and able could do the job.

But when dental colleges sprung up everywhere, fresh graduates from these institutions began the meticulous task of educating the hoi polloi in dental hygiene.

They had to start from scratch, particularly in my home country, India. The application of tree twigs, orange powder and soft ash to scrub the teeth were discouraged. Regular check-ups, and bi-annual visits to the nearest dental clinics became the norm.

We were told about the many bodily diseases that sprung-up by neglecting one's dental health. The mouth was a hotbed of bacteria, and if not routinely checked, could cause inflammation of the arteries. This could lead to high blood pressure, heart disease and even a stroke. If it clogged the veins of the lungs, acute bronchitis or pneumonia would follow.

Anaerobic bacteria cause *halitosis.* It is an ailment that gives rise to foul-smelling breath. As far back as 1500 BC, Egyptian medical writing documented this disorder, and recommended a combination of herbs and wine to counter it.

Ancient Chinese healers suggested that a white coating on the tongue could be the culprit, and invented a tongue cleaner.

Halitosis can be an embarrassing problem, especially in societies where kissing on the cheeks is used as a form of social greeting.

The sufferers are usually unaware of this malady because the air from their mouth does not enter their own noses. In a majority of cases, they have to rely on others to tell them about it.

Recently, I gagged and had to hold my breath while suffering saliva-dripping kisses, from a halitosis-suffering uncle of mine. When he hugged me, I almost fainted.

The thought of handing him my dentist's number flashed briefly before my eyes. "Somebody had to do it, why not me," said the voice in my head.

It was unavoidable so I thought of ways to soften the blow. One has to be cruel to be kind, I reasoned with myself.

But when the time came to say goodbye, I chickened out. Folding my hands in the Indian greeting was an easier option.

"Namaste," I said politely, from a safe distance, before scooting off.

Father Special

Every male becomes a father the day his child is born. It is inevitable, and the transition from boy to man is complete the instant he holds his infant in his arms.

From that moment, he makes a promise: to provide, protect, love and shelter his offspring forever afterwards. It is a salient covenant that he signs, with his inner self. There is no guiding light that compels him to do so. It is simply one more wonder of fatherhood that flows seamlessly from one generation to the next.

In most parts of the globe, the world celebrates Father's Day on a particular day of the year. By honouring dads, they want to mark their significance.

It is a noble thought, no doubt, because in this modern age, loving and respecting your parents is not a given any more and so every relationship has to be acknowledged and celebrated, even the ones that are usually taken for granted. It seems that, these days, feelings have to be expressed, and emotions have to be demonstrated, for them to carry any weight.

Or so say the self-help gurus who would otherwise go out of business.

Fathers and daughters share a special bond. Even though it is more than a decade since I lost my father, just thinking about him brings an instant smile to my lips.

He belonged to the old school of chivalry where men opened

doors for women, and in a restaurant seated them before pulling out their own dining chairs.

Impeccably dressed at all times, my dad had a full-length mirror installed, outside his office. He wanted all the officers to assess their appearance, before coming to work. Alternately, go back home if they were scruffily turned out.

First impressions are important, my father said. One must speak up to be heard, he said. You must follow your dreams, he said.

Appreciation of little things, like the sight of a crimson sunset, the sound of a roaring waterfall or the taste of an alien pudding was heartily encouraged. Basking in his love and affection, there was nothing that I was incapable of doing. It is one of the most wonderful feelings in the world. For tiny girls to know that they have their father's unconditional support, that is.

Lavish and effusive with his praise, my dad could make anyone feel ten feet tall. Everyday, without fail, he would thank my mother at the dinner table for the meals that she prepared.

A natural entertainer, he radiated instantaneous warmth in a crowd, by his infectious laughter. Without the slightest hesitation, he would quote a poem that he had read, or a song he had memorised. Like every other girl, I believed that my father was exceptional.

If I thought my father was a great hero, our daughter thinks her daddy is very special too.

When she was younger, her favourite words were '*Papa look at me*'.

Anything that she achieves, academically or otherwise, has to be positively endorsed by him. The accolades mean more to her, if they made him happy.

She takes his continued interest in her well-being, as a birthright. It is heartwarming to see her treasuring his paternal attention.

Watching them interact is like reliving my own childhood.

The wheel has turned a full circle.

Hanging a Picture

If I had known how well paying a handyman's job was, I would have studied plumbing or carpentry in college.

Even a short crash course in learning how to mend a leaking tap could have been of immense help in fixing showers, pipes, tubs, sprinklers and so on. The list is endless.

Come to think of it, I would be so much in demand that by now a neat pile of my money would be parked in a fancy bank. You know, those places, where everyone moves around in dark suits and talks in hushed whispers.

Somebody should have guided me towards this bit of imaginary wealth, but nobody did.

And so, I missed that opportunity in life. I am now at the receiving end of a handyman's total apathy towards me and my woes.

I don't know about other places, but in Amman, these specialists are highly sought after, with their phones forever emitting a busy tone. Even when you get through to them, their appointment diary is so blocked that if you are lucky, the earliest they come by is three weeks later.

It is easier to get a slot at the dentist than get a handyman over on a house call. This is not to say that the dentists in Jordan are an idle lot. Not at all, it's just that these professionals are busier.

So, most reluctantly I had to go down the DIY route.

What does the abbreviation stand for? For the uninitiated, the three letters signify *'do it yourself'*. Do what yourself? Well, anything and everything to do with carpentering, plumbing or electrician work that the ever-absentee handyman would have done for you, if he ever showed up.

When an international hardware store opened up a branch locally, I couldn't wait to be there. True to its reputation, the shop stocked all that one could possibly think of for putting a house together. Wide aisles clearly marked the various sections, and made it seem like a toy store.

From fancy drill machines, nails, hooks, hammers, tool boxes, ladders, to bathtub plugs, doorstoppers, shelves, collapsible shoeboxes, it had everything and more. With an extremely helpful salesman pushing my shopping cart, I bought things that I didn't even know existed.

Coming in through the front door, I saw that a painting I had ordered previously had been delivered. It was lying propped against a wall. Knowing how long it would take to get a carpenter to pass by and hang it, I thought this would be an ideal opportunity to try out my newly purchased DIY kit.

I recalled *Jerome K Jerome*'s story. I did not want to end up like poor *Uncle Podger* and immediately recruited my housemaid's assistance.

A stepladder was brought and I was carefully assisted in climbing it. A pencil was handed, along with a nail and a hammer.

I marked a point on the wall and positioned a sharp hook precisely.

But the minute I swung the first blow, my doorbell rang.

The maid intuitively ran to answer it, leaving me to wobble precariously on the top step. The ladder or my balance gave way. I found myself bruised and lying in a heap on the floor.

And, without giving away the details, suffice it to say that Aunt Polly (she of the Jerome novel) did eventually hang the picture!

Of Baths and Turkish Baths

Don't get me wrong; I have nothing against baths. Bathing is a wonderful pastime, and very necessary for cleaning and grooming the skin.

But the mystery associated with a good bubble bath is exhilarating. Reminds one of the extremely popular period black and white films, where a killer lurked behind a shower curtain, and waited for a *Marilyn Monroe* type to emerge from the tub, before casually strangling her. Immortal scenes!

The Greeks and Romans built the communal baths called *Hamams*. These were covered areas, with several pools of water in varying degrees of temperature. The bathers immersed themselves into it, following a sequence set out—one could go from a warm bath to a cold one, but not the other way round.

I can't verify that bit of the past, but I know that in Amman there are plenty of places that provide the facility of traditional Turkish baths. The regulars have their own favourite ones, which they frequent routinely.

Recently, I was invited to try out a newly opened one in a local five star hotel.

There was an aqua aerobics class in session in one of the pools when I reached the venue. The instructor was an energetic Australian lady, who obviously enjoyed living in water. Before taking me to the Spa, she made me do some of the warm-up exercises. This

consisted of twisting, and turning of the body, which I managed to do with some effort.

Then I was sprayed with a strong flood of water that gushed through a hosepipe and oozed with such force that it left me gasping for breath. It was to get rid of my unwanted cellulite, I was told. I was ready to give up the entire idea, and run away.

By the time the session ended, I had been soaked for three long hours, and had wrinkled skin from too much water-exposure. I went through the final motions without registering anything. My brain, along with my limbs, had gone numb.

It was an ordeal I never wanted to repeat in my lifetime.

So, when I visited Turkey, I was mentally prepared. Within a couple of days of being in Istanbul, our hosts suggested we try out the Hamam experience. I pretended to be sick, made a polite excuse and refused the offer.

My husband ventured forth bravely, with his friend. They were supposed to come back in one hour but were absent for several.

Eventually, both the men lumbered home through the doorway, walking with obvious discomfort. They looked well scrubbed and their skin was baby pink, almost peeling. They kept drinking more and more glasses of water.

I knew what they were going to say, but I wanted to hear it anyway.

"We were totally fleeced," said spouse.

"And drenched in water for over four hours," his buddy added.

"The attendants were all crooks," my husband muttered.

"We were ill-handled by them," his friend supplied.

"It was sheer torture, and we will never step a toe in bath water again," they chorused.

I think I get it.

Stitch in Time

I was told early in life that: '*a stitch in time saves nine*'.

But to my utter dismay, whenever the moment comes for me to rescue those nine precious stitches, I end up with more than my fair share of problems.

I look up to people who are swift with the needle and thread. I am in total awe of those who can sew, knit, tailor and embroider things to perfection. Actually, folks who can thread the needle at the first go, without fraying the edges, get my complete admiration too.

Jumma, my tailor, is my absolute hero. I place him on a pedestal from where he has no hopes of ever climbing down.

That is because he not only cuts the cloth according to precise designs, but also manages to make superb outfits out of it, complete with embroidery, pleats, buttons and hooks in place. Jumma sews with such dedication that it is a joy to see bits of material being transformed into stylish dresses, by his magical fingers.

But when I met him for the first time, it was a humbling experience. For me, that is.

I had been in the city for all of four months, and everything was still new. I was in the process of integrating into a new culture, peoples and society.

Trying to fix a loose button on my favorite blouse, I had wrestled with the pointed needle for hours. My fingers were sore and blood-ridden and my eyes were seeing double from the sheer concentration.

Giving up the losing battle, I reluctantly made my way to the tiny tailoring shop across the road from my house. Swallowing my pride, I tried to come up with a good reason to explain why I was incapable of fixing the sorry blouse.

Jumma was in his customary place and welcomed me from behind the sewing machine.

"What can I do for you? You want alterations done on the shirt, yes?" he asked me.

"Sort of," I answered.

"You want it tucked in or opened up?" he queried.

"Neither," I mumbled.

Feeling sorry for me, Jumma walked up to the counter, a half stitched dress trailing behind him.

"Actually, I want to get a button fixed," I said in a rush.

"You want it changed? Why didn't you say so? Let me check." Jumma took the blouse from me.

"I simply want one button fixed. I ran out of thread and then I lost the needle," I rambled.

Jumma was not convinced. Seeing the wrinkled cloth around the loose fastening, he gave me a knowing look.

"You tried to sew this yourself? Not good with needlework, are you?" he questioned.

"A complete disaster," I confessed.

"Yes," he agreed.

"First the thread knotted up behind the button and then in front of it. When I cut it, the cloth also came off," I clarified.

Jumma smiled and sewed the button back while explaining the intricacies of keeping the needle from pinching the fingers. He also embroidered a flowery pattern around the bit of cloth I had nicked.

"A stitch in time," he started.

Seeing my horrified expression, he halted in mid sentence.

"Never mind, next time you just bring it here," he instructed.

Like I said before, he is the stuff heroes are made of!

Alarm Bells

Sleeping is very much like a recharging of batteries. It allows our tired bodies to rest, rejuvenate and wake up refreshed. As infants, we sleep most of the time, but on growing older, the sleep cycle diminishes. In some people, it vanishes altogether, turning them into insomniacs.

These folks have to fill their sleepless hours with some other constructive activity, like reading, listening to music or hectic spring-cleaning.

For most of us, going to sleep is not a problem. It is the waking up that is difficult, especially when one has to catch an early morning flight.

Therefore, the most prized possession for any busy traveller like me is the alarm clock. Where timepieces are concerned, I don't have anything against them. However, for a variety of reasons, I have not taken to alarm clocks.

That is because these devices have a tendency to start ringing when you are in the deepest part of your sleep phase. You know, the one that is scientifically described as non-rapid eye movement or NREM.

Moreover, even though I keep it on my bedside before going to sleep, when the time comes to switch the ringer off, the clock seems to have moved, more than a foot away.

How does that happen? I don't know. But I have to get up to grope for the timer in the dark, and switch the sound off. Sometimes,

by the time this is done, not just me, but my entire household, is roused into wakefulness.

My husband, and other well-meaning people have told me to awaken my internal clock. Also known as the circadian rhythm, this, apparently, is a biological clock inbuilt within all of us. It instinctively guides us on when to sleep or wake up.

One just programmes the timing in one's head, and *abracadabra,* the body responds into sharp wakefulness in the morning. Just like that.

After learning of its various advantages, I decided to rouse my internal clock immediately. Armed with all the information I could find, I got down to work.

At bedtime, I methodically ticked everything on the mental exercise chart that the self-help book guided me to. The last step, where I had to press my head seven times on a pillow for a seven o'clock wake up call to myself, was a little silly. But I did it anyway.

At midnight I woke up with a start. Peering into my wristwatch I saw that it was too early to arise, and went back to sleep. After approximately one hour, my malfunctioning internal clock gave me another sudden jolt. I checked the time, and found that it was still not sunrise, and groggily closed my eyes again.

I was woken up repeatedly at two, three and four o'clock, and in this disruptive manner, I spent the rest of the night.

By morning I was convinced that my internal clock was either missing or totally beyond repair.

But how did spouse manage it?

One minute before seven, I heard a sharp clicking noise. This was a precursor to the alarm. It emerged from my sleeping partner's side of the bed. My husband reached out sneakily, and pressed the snooze button, on its very first ring.

Aha, a surreptitious alarm bell?

Moustache Tales

In Asia and the Middle East, one comes across a wide variety of moustaches.

It is not that moustachioed males are not spotted in other parts of the globe, but it appears to be a particular specialty of this specific region. It is rather a norm than an aberration here.

Almost every man sports this fashion accessory, in isolation, or as an accompaniment to a beard.

My research tells me that the moustache, which is explained as ungroomed growth of hair over the upper lip of males, was initially used to intimidate enemies during battle. In antiquity, they believed that it added to the ferociousness of the facial expression.

These days there are still members of the older generation and particular cultures (think of South Indian film stars) who seem to associate moustaches with authority. On the contrary, the metrosexual youth of today regards facial hair, which was considered a sign of wisdom, virility and masculinity, as a certain lack of refinement.

There are different types of moustaches: from the bushy to the pointy, the twirl up types, and the droopy ones. Some resemble the shape of a sleeping caterpillar, while others look like handlebars. There are pencil, tapered and toothbrush moustaches, and the ones that look like a horseshoe.

I have also observed that men who wear this hairy bit of growth on their face have some compulsive mannerisms to go with it. Most often, they are found twitching the ends of their moustache, between their thumb and forefinger.

It is almost as if they want to make sure of its presence. Or maybe it is a covert manner of brushing off the crumbs of food and drink that get stuck onto it.

Some moustaches look like the gentleman forgot to shave in the morning. But on closer inspection, it is revealed that barbers from swanky salons of metropolitan cities are the ones responsible for carefully cultivating this look.

Exceptionally talented, these experts offer consultation on how to grow and maintain a moustache. They trim, tease, colour and tweeze the hair growth, and make sure the moustache is appropriately shaped for every occasion. There is never a hair out of place under their watch. From a Clark Gable to a Cary Grant look, they manufacture it all with a snip of their sharp scissors.

Not being a man, and never having worn a moustache, I have always wondered what makes men want to live with this excessive growth on their faces.

Doesn't the fine hair tickle their nostrils and make them sneeze? Is it not a problem while brushing their teeth? In summer months, does the sweat not make it itchy? Can one smile easily from behind a moustache? And most importantly, is it not a hindrance in amorous adventures?

The only time my spouse grew a moustache was when he was refused entry from the bar of a club because he looked underage. Smarting with humiliation, he stopped shaving his upper lip. A few weeks later, he surfaced with a debonair-looking moustache, and was welcomed with open arms.

For the last decade or so, he has been clean-shaven. But the other day, he was once again denied admission into a trendy joint called 'Forty Plus'.

History was repeating itself.

Eager to help him, I have hidden his razor.

Name Calling

William Shakespeare posed an interesting question in the sixteenth century.

Actually, he made one of the protagonists of his play come up with the query.

'What's in a name? That which we call a rose,
By any other name would smell as sweet.'
Romeo and Juliet (*Act II, Scene II*)

The Bard set the ball rolling with this enquiry but several centuries later we have still not found a sufficiently clear answer to it.

Is there really nothing to a name? If we interchange one name with the other, would it signify the same thing?

For instance: were we to call a rose, cauliflower, would it still smell as sweet? To superimpose the bland image of a cauliflower onto a rose is blasphemous, but if we stretched our imagination and managed it, would the fragrance linger?

I don't have an answer to that, but what I do know is, where personal names are concerned, societies follow different patterns. In some cultures, parents like to honour the elders in the family and name their children after them. In other parts of the world, people like to give unusual names to their offspring or melodious sounding ones. Some peruse the religious texts and provide godlike names to their progeny.

Indians have an interesting custom. In my home country, all of us have two names. One is the formal one, which is imparted

with much fanfare in our infancy. The second is called a 'pet name'. This is a somewhat shortened version of our proper name. At times, it is just a comic term that a hapless child is carelessly labelled with.

So, we might have a six-footer strapping man called 'Tiny' or a sixty-year-old lady named 'Baby'. A thin person could be called 'Fatty,' or a pessimistic one 'Happy'.

In certain families, kids are named in matching rhyme, like Kikki, Ricki, Vikki, Tikki and Mikki. Very unimaginative, but easy to remember, I am told.

When I was younger, all I wanted to do, and quite desperately, was to change my name. My father had gone to great lengths to find an unusual one for me, but I simply hated it.

In school, especially during roll call, my teachers would pause when they reached me, and would ask for the meaning of my unfamiliar name. I would blush with embarrassment, and try to clarify, to the best of my ability, something that I could not understand myself.

My siblings teased me mercilessly. They gave imaginatively nasty twists to my name daily. I would be reduced to tears and refused to answer when they called out to me.

Every week, I would fervently try and switch my name to: Rose, Kate, Anna or Tara. But, gradually, I began to accept my name for what it was.

Recently, quite unexpectedly, I was given a fresh shock. An Internet website claimed that the interpretation of my name was not *'Bouquet of flowers'* after all. I was actually a *'Garden of creepers'*.

If the former name-calling was bad, the latter was worse.

In desperation, I turned towards Shakespeare. The Bard obliged with a helpful list.

Therefore, with immediate effect, I have now decided to call myself: *Juliet.*

Bad Hair Day

Where accuracy of future predictions is concerned, I firmly believe in only one of them.

No, it is not the daily horoscope, or the philosophical forecast that emerges when you crack open a fortune cookie. Nothing as exotic as that, I'm afraid.

I can precisely foresee how my day is going to be, just by looking at hair. The hair on my own head, that is.

It involves the most basic of daily routines. All I have to do after waking up is walk towards my toothbrush, and steal a glance at the mirror. In my younger years, this used to reproduce a better-looking likeness, I must admit. But here I digress.

So, viewing the reflection unblinkingly, one of the three scenarios is presented. The first is when the hair on my head looks smooth and shiny, swinging like soft silk, gently on my shoulders.

This cheers me up, because it is an immediate precursor to a fantastic day. I am ready to handle all challenges. There is a spring in my step and a song on my lips. Nothing seems impossible to me. I am willing to climb the tallest mountain, swim the widest sea.

Second scenario is my hesitant gaze discovering wisps of listless tresses, floating in a frizzy zigzag, around my head. At such a sighting, I whip out a roller brush and try to bring some order to the chaos. Sometimes I am successful, and manage to tame the unruly locks into normalcy.

My day, accordingly, suffers. It might start off nicely, but midway, turns and goes downhill. Or, after suffering a dull start, it suddenly takes off on a bright cloud.

In other words, it is most unpredictable. On days like these, you will not find me skipping around, but I am not dragging my feet either.

The final type is, when I get up, and even before reaching for the toothpaste, the mirror announces the bad news. And my hair actually looks like it belongs to an alien head.

In front of my disbelieving eyes, I see it sticking out like straw, pointing in every wild direction. No amount of pacifying shampoo or conditioner helps, because, on such days, every tendril on my head is obstinately immune. If I try twisting it one way, it stubbornly curls into an opposite angle.

The phrase *Bad hair day* was coined for something like this.

It is a better idea to go right back to bed and sleep off the rest of the day, rather than blunder along. Everything goes wrong when you venture out, and if you don't take it seriously, there is no way to avoid the misfortune that is waiting to happen.

I confided all of this to my old school friend whom I met recently after a span of several decades. Back then he had a shock of bushy unruly black hair, with a beard to match. But now, he was wearing a cap through which he kept nodding at me.

As I paused for breath, he pulled the top hat off, and I saw a smooth bald head, where his locks used to be.

"There is a fourth category too," he announced.

"Ahem!" I tried to cover the embarrassment.

"No confusion, and you are always light-headed," he stated.

"I can't guess," I said.

"No hair day," he declared, laughing uproariously.

Green Bangles

Of all the various pieces of jewellery that women adorn themselves with, bangles are the noisiest.

The bells in anklets make a tinkling sound too, I grant that. Even if one tries to tiptoe around as noiselessly as possible, they give your presence away.

But the jingling noise that an armful of bangles make is simply inimitable. They not only announce your own whereabouts, but if you tune your ear carefully, they allow you to gauge the exact proximity of another bangle-wearer too.

In South Asian countries, bangles, which are usually favoured by women, but in this modern age, often by men too, signify various things, from the marital status of a lady to the affluence of her background. The more wealthy ones, for instance, like to wear bangles made of gold, diamonds and other precious stones.

Though bangles can be carved out of silver, iron, seashells, copper, plastic, and even wood, there is nothing to beat the charm of glass bangles. There is an old-fashioned romance associated with it that is impossible to explain. Both the bangle wearer, as well as the bangle seller, is woven intrinsically into it.

When I was small, during the festive season, the glass bangle sellers would arrive at our doorstep religiously. They carried a jute basket over their heads, from which emerged large bundles loosely tied in cotton cloth. These would be untied slowly and mysteriously,

to uncover an array of the most beautiful glass bangles, in a multitude of colours.

My mother was a busy housewife and did not like to be disturbed while completing her household chores. I, meanwhile, had all the time in the world to chat with these interesting vendors. Most of them were grey-haired and elderly but what kept me riveted to their side, was the lively chatter.

I was not a hyper child, but my over protective mum and grandmother did not let me get too close to anything that was made of glass or porcelain and was easily breakable.

The bangle sellers, on the other hand, allowed me to crawl into their huge basket, and pick out any glass bangle that I wanted. I could slip it on my arm, where it would slide immediately onto my shoulder. Or hold it against the sunlight, and squint at its radiance.

They embellished their sale with colourful stories, and told me that when I grow up, I should only wear green-coloured bangles. Always.

Surprisingly, just recently, on a trip to a city, which is famous for glass bangles, I experienced an uncanny echo of this scene.

"Try some Indian bangles," an old saleslady called out to me.

I smiled in response.

"Is this your first visit to this country?" she asked again.

"Not really. I was born here," I confided.

"You are Indian? Why are you not wearing bangles then?" she scolded. "With your colouring green bangles will suit you," she announced.

"But why only green?" I finally asked the question.

"Because it will ward off the evil eye. Let me take care of you," she chuckled.

She sold me so many bangles that now I can open my own shop.

I will call it: *The green trap.*

Compulsive Obsession

What a wonderfully scientific world we live in these days, where medical advancement has ensured that we have longer, pain free lives.

Most of the diseases can be diagnosed and treated by the skills of the physicians and surgeons.

Jordan is a country, which is especially popular as a healthcare hub in the Middle East, where scores of patients troop in on a regular basis. The doctors are brilliant and have a cure for all types of bodily ailments.

There is no dearth of psychologists and psychiatrists too. The shrinks, as they are commonly called in colloquial slang, are people who look after our mental well-being. So if one is suffering from depression, melancholy, despair or an unexplained bout of sadness, one seeks them out.

I liked the idea of visiting a shrink. The closest I have ever come to one is via a Woody Allen movie, the majority of which have scenes in psychiatrist's offices.

The doctor usually sits behind a desk, while the patient reclines on a couch-like sofa, and talks. Occasionally, he jots down notes on a writing pad, and if the conversation subsides, he prods the talker with pertinent queries.

I enjoyed this portrayal of psychologists, I really did. I mean I lived in a house where nobody had the inclination to listen to my complaints. And here was a person whose sole occupation was to hear me out. I could not wait to get myself to a shrink. All I needed was an appropriate ailment, which would help me get an appointment with one of them.

I am not an unhappy person, so depression was ruled out. I do not have much patience for melancholia and sadness also. But I am a perfectionist and like to keep my home and hearth spotlessly neat and clean.

I did not think this was a negative quality, but if I presented it as an obsessive-compulsive disorder, maybe the doctor would give me that much needed chitchat session on the couch.

Moreover, I was fascinated with the words, *obsession* and *compulsion*. The former meant being continuously preoccupied with a fixed idea, feeling or emotion. The latter was an irresistible urge to behave in a particular manner despite the consequences. I admired obsessive compulsion. Why was the *disorder* term associated with it? I needed to find that out.

Next day I called up the clinic. At the scheduled hour, I presented myself at the hospital. The doctor made me sit at his desk while he excused himself to make a call.

I saw that his table was cluttered with knick-knacks. Before I could stop myself, I tidied it all up, putting the magazines in a neat stack, pens in the pen-stand and the used coffee cup in the side tray.

"What are you doing?" asked the shrink, when he walked back.

"Putting things in order," I smiled.

"Why?" he inquired.

"It was messy, so I cleared it," I replied.

"It was my mess," he said belligerently.

"But it was on my side of the table," I insisted.

"Confirmed OCD," he stated.

"You or me?" I muttered under my breath.

"What did you say?" he thundered.

"Nothing! I have to go, sorry," I said, rushing out.

Affectionate Display

These days it is all about how you market yourself.

The world is not interested in knowing you as you are, but perceives you, as you want to be perceived. Everything is contrived and nothing is left to the imagination. Even emotions are manufactured and marketable.

So, if you love someone, it is not just enough to care for the person deeply but one has to visibly show it, in a hundred different ways.

Like buying gifts, remembering birthdays, addressing each other in mushy endearments, calling up constantly, and last but not the least, engaging in public displays of affection. The entire amorous industry thrives on manipulating us in this manner.

There is no such thing as privacy anymore. Private, which is loosely defined as something secluded from the sight, presence or intrusion of others, is an alien term. With the advent of the social networking sites, one gets to know such extreme detail, about so many people, that it is staggering.

But it was not always like this. I remember the age of subtlety.

Things were not perfect then. Telephones often did not work, cars were not air-conditioned, roads were pot-holed and a journey of a few miles took a large part of our day. But there was romance, so much of it.

People had ample free time, and there was a delicacy and refinement to every little thing. For instance, picnics or trips to the movies were organised in minute detail. From the table linen,

crockery and cutlery, to the food menu, all of it was meticulously planned and discussed. An entourage would be sent a day earlier, to secure a picnic spot, or purchase the film tickets.

In a majority of cases, a professional photographer was also invited. Scenes of revelry would be captured in his lens, and postcards were made out of the clicked pictures. These were later converted into season's greetings cards, and circulated amongst friends.

There was a gentle nuance to romantic love also. Lovers took great pains to keep their beloved's identity a secret, and never announced their besotted state publicly. Love was something to be felt and experienced between two individuals, and not for the voyeuristic pleasure of all and sundry.

My own parents, who adored one another, followed certain decorum in their conversation, and spoke to each other most respectfully.

Being from such a background, when I got married, the first thing I wanted to hide, were my colourful wedding bangles, which proclaimed to the world my status as a new bride. My shyness made me stumble over the newly acquired wedded surname also.

Over the years I managed to overcome quite a few of my inhibitions. But public display of affection was still unfamiliar to me.

The other day, the flight I was traveling in took a sudden plunge. In sheer nervousness I closed my eyes and clutched my husband's hand, for reassurance.

"Are you alright?" spouse inquired in an amused voice.

"Are we still alive?" I asked, without opening my eyes.

"If you keep pinching my hand like that, one of us might not be," he laughed.

"Sorry," I said moving away immediately.

"Don't be, there might be more turbulence, who can tell?" he grinned, grabbing my hand right back.

Safety first?

Khanna Aunty's Room

Huge rambling mansions remind me of the days of my childhood. The bungalows we lived in had more rooms than inhabitants. The British got them built, during the Raj, and after independence, native officers inherited those dwellings. My father was one of them.

But by the time we moved in, the fireplaces, all several of them, had developed cracks, and there were gaps in the ceiling, from which rainwater would trickle onto my mum's expensive carpets. They were not actually so costly, now that I think about it. Those rugs on the ground, that is. It is just that on a government employee's salary, she would painstakingly save money for many months, in order to buy these small luxuries. And once she purchased them, they acquired the statues of family heirlooms.

And the house rules, ah the house rules! We could not walk indoors with muddy shoes, dirty sandals or wet slippers. In fact, it was safest to keep a secure distance, and generally tiptoe around gingerly, on silent feet.

So, you can imagine the ruckus that was caused in my home, every time raindrops had the audacity to fall on these floor coverings. There would be chaos, even if it were the middle of the night, with frenetic activity involving plastic sheets, mops and buckets.

Everyone would emerge from his or her room, to take part in this rescue mission. And we had plenty of those, like I said before, some of them locked up because of non-occupancy. Other than the dining, drawing, living, sleeping, lounging, bathing and kitchen, we had several guest rooms too.

There is a cheeky word in my mother tongue Hindi, which is called, '*faltu*'. Its exact translation is 'unwanted'. I know it has a somewhat negative connotation, but our domestic staff would have no qualms about using the term.

If a guest walked in unexpectedly, they would announce, 'Faltu Sahib is here,' without batting an eyelid. They would then proceed to ask if they should prepare the 'unwanted room' for the 'unwanted visitor'.

Even as a child, I would get embarrassed at such blatantly rude references to our poor unsuspecting callers. But these domestics, trained by their erstwhile employers, were simply immune to my pleadings.

When I got married, for the initial decade or so, I lived in flats, where a couple of rooms were all we had. And so there was no point in earmarking anything with specific designations.

Then we moved to a huge villa where, after allocating the usual quarters, we still had three extra guest compartments. One I turned into my study, but the other two were crying out for a name.

Khanna Aunty was our first visitor here. An elegantly grey-haired, wonderful lady, she arrived from Delhi to celebrate her seventieth birthday with us. I loved her company and promptly christened the chamber she was staying in, as Khanna Aunty's room. It helped to distinguish it from the other parts of the house, and there was less confusion all around.

Next, we got relocated to Jordan. As the packers unloaded the boxes, I saw several pieces marked as Aunt K, in bold ink.

"These will go into Auntie's room," declared one burly un-packer.

"Which one?" I asked.

"You don't know your own Aunty?" he was horrified.

"She does not live here," I clarified.

"Why not?" he queried.

"Never mind! At least Khanna Aunty's room travels with us, just put it there," I directed.

Peace and Beyond

In the third world countries, you can get by without knowing a lot of things.

There is never any need to learn every skill because in these places what is lacking in infrastructure is more than made up by its sheer manpower. So, if you are saddled with any task, there are several people who can perform it for you.

Take this scenario for instance: your car breaks down in the middle of a road. The tyre has to be changed or, worse still, it has to be towed away.

Do you have to roll up your sleeves and get down to the chore? Not at all! Individuals will materialise out of thin air, to offer help. A bit of money exchanges hands and, before you know it, everything is fixed.

You simply get used to this kind of behaviour, and you become quite useless at helping your own self. This in itself makes for embarrassing moments, when you travel abroad and something as simple as opening a sauce bottle becomes a major challenge.

The people in the country you have journeyed to cannot understand why you are so inept, especially if you look able bodied and mentally stable and they have never visited your homeland.

For me, individually, self-help is an alien concept. I never get a chance, you see. There are so many people eager to help me that I am the last person I turn towards.

Perhaps it has something to do with my diminutive stature. I

would add meek nature, but even under the cover of poetic license, that would be an untruthful description of myself, I realise that. But what I cannot fathom is why people are so keen to rush to my aid.

Therefore, when I walk into bookstores and see shelves lined with books on self-help, I don't even go there. I mean what is the point? Of teaching myself the art of flower arrangement, cooking cabbage soup, or gardening, that is.

But one day I came across the term '*inner peace*'. It was during a *Deepak Chopra* talk.

This wily new age guru was a holistic, alternative medicine practitioner, physician, public speaker, and writer all rolled into one. I was a part of his captivated audience.

My first question to him when I met him in person was, how to find the reclusive *inner peace* that he preached about.

"See, it is simple. When anyone is confused, their inner harmony becomes a mythical goal, and troubled thoughts or unhappy feelings cannot be turned into reconciliation," he told me.

"Huh?" I said.

"Yes," he smiled.

"You are going to help me find it, right?" I requested.

"The secret of your peaceful equilibrium is that it already exists," he stated.

"Where?" I was curious.

"It is within you. You just have to uncover this discovery," he insisted.

"How?" I asked.

"Like blowing dust off a mirror," he lectured.

"Phoo, phoo, like this?" I inquired puffing my cheeks out.

"Exactly," he replied.

Legendary Tales

I have always been a bookworm.

I have no qualms about admitting that. Story books fascinate me and the written word mesmerizes me. On any given day, I like to curl up with a book and get lost in the imaginary world that it conjures up.

But the sad thing is nobody has the time or patience for people with an imaginative bent of mind. As a quality, it is greatly undervalued these days, and not many folks understand how creativity can transform everything.

When our daughter was a toddler, whenever she was ill or bedridden, I would invent games for her. Her favourite one was when I would switch on the TV, tune it into some political discussion or dramatic serial, and turn down the volume. The rule was that the two of us provided the voice over.

The fun started in earnest, when we improvised the scenes impulsively, and made the reporters speak completely bizarre dialogues.

The President of a country, for example, could be reading out a State of the Union Address, but with our imaginative dubbing he/she would be giving tips on gardening or hair transplant. If there were a tragic scene going on, we would juxtapose it with a comic one, or vice versa.

We would compete with each other, in total seriousness. But within moments, my little patient would dissolve into peals of laughter. And we would have to start from scratch, all over again.

Conceiving innovative endings to a fairy tale, instead of the predictable ones, was another contest. You know, like if Cinderella's glass slipper did not fit her, then what? Or, if the frog prince continued to be a frog, even after the princess kissed him, what would happen then?

The child came up with hilarious suppositions. The wicked witch would turn into one of her dreaded schoolteachers, and the unfortunate lassie would discover her hidden talent, and go on to write *the Misplaced Slipper* series, which would make her a millionaire.

With the passage of time, my daughter went away to college and I started reading out stories to the kids in our neighbourhood. They would sit around in rapt attention, and look at me with unblinking eyes. The greater the twist I added to a tale, the more they enjoyed listening to it.

Soon, I dabbled with the idea of writing a children's book. I wanted to document a collection of fables that the little ones could read, for themselves.

As soon as I voiced this thought, I had people offering me free suggestions. I have heard of the cart jumping the horse, but here it was an entire bandwagon that was hopping, skipping and leaping, in front of the proverbial mule.

The most excited about this project, was my immediate family. They not only wanted me to write a book quickly, but wished to be prominently featured in it, as well.

"So have you thought of a title yet?" my husband questioned me the other day

"For what?" I asked.

"Call your book, *Living with a Legend*," he suggested.

"I am not a legend," I said, horrified.

"That would be me, so name it, *Married to a Legend*," he specified.

"You are not a legend," I muttered, frowning.

"You can make us into one Mom, call it, *Mother of a Legend*," our daughter piped up.

Mistaken legends? Or, Legendary mistakes? Who can tell?

Diary of an Over-thinker

Thinking in small doses is a harmless pastime.

Here one employs one's mind objectively in order to form an opinion, or evaluate a situation. This is rational behaviour, and, under no circumstance, should it be condoned.

The problem arises when your thoughts go on an over-drive. And, instead of reaching a reasonable conclusion, you arrive at an inconclusive sort of dead-end. For want of a better term, I call such people *over-thinkers*, and to my utter surprise, I found myself fitting into this category.

To correct this bit of foolishness before it developed into a nasty habit, I decided to write a diary. Putting my thoughts, albeit frenzied and jumbled-up ones, on paper, could help me train myself. To think in a crystal-clear manner, that is.

Not finding a conventional journal at hand, I put a writing-pad that I had pinched from a hotel and a pencil, on my bedside table. At various intervals throughout the day I made hasty entries into it.

Neither my domestic staff nor my family could understand why I needed to trudge to my room every few hours to scribble something into a sheet of paper.

Raised eyebrows and odd looks came my way, but I ignored them all. Training needs discipline, and to coach something, as intangible as one's own over-thinking required all the strictness I could muster, I told myself.

My first entry of the day read: woke up to troubled thoughts.

I was tempted to describe them, but I stopped myself and left it at that. There was a niggling feeling that tried to pull me back, but I snapped out of it, literally and figuratively.

Systematically, I kept jotting down my numerous activities during the day. I also recorded the accompanying mental commotion, in a concise manner, without going into too much of detail.

Opening the notepad late at night, I was pleased with my self-discipline. I was cured of overthinking I thought. One day is all it took. I was so happy with this discovery, that I invited my husband to read out my diary.

"Burnt the cake," he recited, in a clear voice.

"Slightly singed," I corrected him.

"Fought with the gardener," he continued.

"Yes, I fired him today," I said.

"Why?" he was curious.

"He beat up his wife," I explained.

"Ah that is terrible!" he exclaimed.

"Go on," I prompted.

"A missed call at noontime," he read.

I tried desperately to hold on to my wayward thoughts and did not answer for a few moments. In retrospect, I remember I even took a deep breath to calm myself down. And then the dam burst.

"Gosh! Where was the call from? Why did the name not show up along with the number? Who was trying to get in touch with me? Maybe it was something important, a life or death situation?"

"If it was so crucial, the caller would have called back. In fact, he should have called back. Perhaps I ought to have dialled the number? Why didn't I do that?"

"It could be possible that someone important was trying to contact me. Were my friends in trouble? Dear God, please let them be safe," I babbled.

"The more things change, the more they stay the same," announced my husband.

Anger Games

It is easy to find angry people around you.

There are so many of them, seething with rage, that it is a wonder our planet has not gone up in smoke. Scenes of anger are visible everywhere, whichever way you turn.

On the roads are the horn-tooting motorists whizzing past and overtaking you from the wrong side. If the flights or trains are delayed, the passengers hop in pure indignation. In the shopping centers, restaurants, movie halls, hospitals, hotels and even educational institutions, the sound of fury is unmistakable.

Anger, as one understands it, is an emotional response to one's psychological interpretation of having been offended, wronged or denied. It is a feeling of great annoyance or antagonism as a result of some real or perceived grievance.

In other words, are a whole lot of people antagonistic because of false interpretation? And if the wrong perception is corrected, will they cool down?

In my childhood, I did not come across too many wrathful people. I was raised in a small town, whose inhabitants had patience and empathy in large doses.

The closest I came to the term 'anger' was when one Indian movie by the unlikely name of: *Why does Mr. Pinto get angry,* was released. As far as quirky named pictures go, this one was a sure winner. People flocked to the theater just to find an answer to the question.

My parents were cheerful and mild-mannered folks. My mother was the stricter one but even she was more firm than furious, while disciplining us. My father had all the time in the world for us, and each interaction with him was laced in humour.

I remember going to him with a math question when I was seven years old. He looked at me in complete surprise and absent-mindedly asked me when I had started school. He then drew a large kitty in my notebook, and wrote my name on top of it.

"You go and colour this picture. The time for problem solving can wait," he told me.

It was only when I started living in big cities that I encountered real rage. The weirdest part of this was the anger that strangers exhibited towards, well, strangers.

Next, I learned about the term 'fake fury'. Loosely described, this is a false, dramatic rage that people work themselves up to, in order to get out of a sticky situation. An example of this is if you are caught speeding and you act out completely enraged, there is a chance you might be let off, without a ticket.

I took in this information hesitantly, because I did not believe in anger games. But the other day I surprised myself. I had stopped my car on a no-parking zone, by mistake. The traffic warden was at my window in an instant.

"That green van took my place," I accused, even before he could say anything.

"Driving license please?" the cop requested.

"Why don't you fine the van driver?" I asked, frowning.

"Don't teach me my job," the officer said firmly.

"You are yelling at me? You see an innocent lady driver and want to fine her because some awful inconsiderate man bullied his way into her parking?" I screamed.

"Oh, Ok! Just go, go," he waved me away.

"It works," I muttered, hiding my smile.

Virtual Friends

Breaking up is hard to do.

Artists like Paul Anka, Tom Jones, the Carpenters and Gloria Estefan have, over the years, sung this Neil Sedaka number that was first released in 1962.

At various intervals, it was declared the '*most requested song*' of the decade. And more than fifty years down the line the rhythm, music, lyrics and the tune have withstood the test of time.

Breaking up might be difficult, but making new friends is the easiest thing to do, especially in today's virtual world. The social networking sites have opened the floodgates and suddenly, there is a deluge of contacts.

People who have known me as a toddler, schoolgirl, teenager, bride, mother or a book-clubber, have all, sort of, appeared together. To claim me, that is.

The virtual world is an uneasy place. It is impossible to define because it's so full of contradictions. Look at the many definitions of *virtual*, to start off with.

Something that has the appearance and behaviour of the real thing, but is not actually the real thing; existing in essence or effect but not in actual fact, form or name; present in the mind, as a product of the imagination, etc.

Going by these explanations, all things virtual, whether friends, conversations or communities, are entirely imaginary.

Right! If we know the reality of the unreality, so to speak, why

are all the people hooked onto this artificial space? It is like the most philosophical of questions, which no one has yet got an answer for.

Such thoughts trouble me every time I get one more friend request on Facebook, Twitter, LinkedIn, Pinterest or Instagram. There is Flickr, Class Mates and Tagged where folks keep inviting me too. I mean, hardly a day goes by when complete strangers do not overwhelm me with invitations.

Where do all these people come from? It is almost as if whoever I have interacted with since the day I was born has discovered me in the cyber world. It's crazy but true. For a shy and reticent person like me, this is a nightmare.

Individuals who have resisted joining the social networking sites, yes, some of them do exist, do not understand the magnetic pull that it exercises on the rest of us.

My husband is not on Facebook and the other day I wanted to show him some pictures that our daughter had posted on my wall.

"You have seven hundred friends!" spouse exclaimed.

"Six hundred and ninety eight actually," I clarified.

"Who is Yun Che?" he asked

"I don't know, please see the photographs," I said trying to change the subject.

"Is that name for real? Happy Kaur?" he continued.

"No idea. Do you want to see the snaps or not?" I frowned.

"You don't recognise your own friends?" my husband was zapped.

"Yes, er, No," I muttered.

"What did you say?" he probed.

"Breaking up is hard to do," I sang.

"You are crazy," he declared.

"No, er, yes," I agreed.

Telephone Manners

It's been such a hectic day today.

Since morning, all I have done is talk to answering machines. You know, the ones that automatically switch-on after the first ten or twelve beeps, when you are making a call. On the phone, that is.

Talking on the telephone or staying connected is a no-brainer. Every Tom, Dick and Harry as well as their entire tribe of sisters, have a mobile. From florists, cobblers, bakers and cabbies to barbers, grocers, housewives and ten-year-old kids, an entire spectrum of humanity, carry a cellphone with them, wherever they go.

But we know that in reality, this is all balderdash. Owning a phone is very different from getting to speak to the owner of the phone. In most cases, all one gets to do is leave messages on the answering machine.

Soon after Alexander Graham Bell invented the telephone, it made its appearance in the black and white films of the time. *Dial M for Murder*, for instance, had a ringing telephone as its main protagonist. Later movies, especially in the Indian sub continent, had actors sing entire songs to their beloveds over the handset.

Dialling or receiving trunk calls was a laborious process. The sound over the wires would not be clear, and we had to shout in an unnaturally loud voice to get ourselves heard. Telephone manners, which were drilled upon us in early childhood, would invariably come into play.

So, however bad the connection, we had to first greet each

other. Then we had to ask about one another's health, our family's welfare, and inquire about the weather. Only then, could we get down to the point of the call. Sometimes, while bantering about the inconsequential things, the line would get disconnected and the main plot would be lost.

It was back to placing the call and, once connected, going through the pleasantries, one more time. Occasionally, the inquisitive operators, who would be listening in, would sever the link if they felt that the social niceties were not being adhered to.

The greatest allure, still, was in the interaction itself. We would, argue, implore, entreat and quarrel with the telephone receptionists but at least they were human, and not the mechanical recordings of an answering machine.

I cannot understand why people leave messages on the answering machines. If truth be told, I can't even comprehend the instructions that the computerised voice commands me to do. The alien accents trouble me. Also, the false gaiety and cheerfulness that it exudes sets my teeth on edge. By the time I frame a reply in my head and get down to articulating it, the beeps start ringing, loudly.

This morning, for example, I called up an airlines office. A nasal mechanised voice picked up. She told me to press certain numbers but I bungled up immediately. Fuming furiously, I reached the 'leave a message' stage in our conversation, before hanging up.

One hour later, my phone rang.

"How can we solve your problem?" requested a robotic voice.

"Answering machines can make calls too?" I asked, surprised.

"You left a message today," she said.

"No, I didn't," I replied.

"I can play the recording for you," she insisted.

"Really? What did I say?" I was curious.

"Bloody hell! These idiotic scoundrels…" she started reciting.

"Ok, ok, let's get to the point," I cut in.

Scary robots!

Stiff Neck

I've been mulling over a do or not-do choice; a should I, or should I not, type of dilemma; a feeling of being at the crossroads, where one path is a well traversed one, while the other is tantalisingly unknown.

Let me tell you what I would have done a few years back. In my youth I would have unhesitatingly trod the unfamiliar route, without even slowing my stride.

Fools rush in where angels fear to tread idiom fitted me to a 't'. My inherent curiosity about everything and everybody, coupled with an optimistic belief in the goodness of humanity, held me in good stead.

In innumerable instances, I walked up to people in high offices and confronted them if that was necessary. Similarly, I questioned ordinary folks, without a prior introduction, and got startlingly candid home truths from them.

There were no fences that could block my passage, nor any locked doors that punctured my enthusiasm. I pretty much did what my gut instinct guided me to do, and was always rewarded with a myriad of rich experiences.

But motherhood and advancing maturity brought a certain uncertainty in me. Making snap judgments, which was a norm earlier, became increasingly difficult. The moment I decided on one thing, especially for my child, the other option seemed better. I began to weigh the pros and cons, several times over.

So, when the pain in my neck did not recede after swallowing numerous painkillers and applying layers upon layers of Tiger balm, I looked for an alternative treatment. The cervical collar seemed like a good option.

It would help keep the neck immobilised. It would also hold the head up high. My stiff neck was destroying my posture and this could improve it. Maybe. It could possibly add a few more inches to my diminutive frame, which, I was convinced, had reduced when I hung my head to one side.

But with the new indecisiveness that I had adopted lately, I could not come to any decision about whether to buy it or not. I understood that it was silly to cling to vanity in such a situation. Yet, the repugnant collar was just so aesthetically unpleasing, that there was no way to cleverly conceal it. All I needed was a leash as an attachment, and I would resemble a cranky, eccentric domesticated pet. The only saving grace was that at least I did not have whiskers.

"You should definitely try it," said the voice in my head. Before I could change my mind, I drove myself to the nearest pharmacy. The person behind the counter spoke to me in a clipped British accent.

"Good weather, yes?" he greeted me.

"Yes, fantastic," I nodded.

"How can I help you dear lady?" he drawled.

"I have a stiff neck," I complained.

"Better than a stiff upper lip," he said with deadpan expression.

"Will a cervical collar give me relief?" I asked.

"Yes, of course," he nodded.

"But it will look like an eyesore," I complained.

"You can always stitch pearls into it," he suggested.

"Or diamonds," I bluffed.

"Every woman's best friend," he twinkled.

"I wish," I sighed, buying the collar.

Brain Scattered

For the last half an hour I have been moving round and round aimlessly.

I traced my steps and then retraced them, but all to no avail. My reading glasses are misplaced and I am blinded without them. Other than the headlines in the newspapers, I cannot read a thing. And I can't hear very well, either.

I know there is no connection between seeing and hearing. There should not be. Otherwise my ear, nose and throat consultant and eye specialist would be one and the same person. I would save a lot of time and energy flitting from one clinic to another.

But strangely, when I see fuzzily, I hear woozily also.

It is amazing how, the minute my spectacles are balanced on my nose, there is instant clarity to my vision, hearing, inhaling, exhaling and all the rest of it. Even my faded-jaded memory comes to life, and I can recall in photographic detail whatever needs to be recollected. But without them I am lost.

Generally, I find them in the usual place, which is at the top of my head. That is where I push them when I am looking at something quite a distance away. But when the top of my head is empty, and a cursory glace at the mirror doubly confirms it, I get panic stricken.

Then there is absolutely no telling where I could have carelessly abandoned the specs. In my family, the tales of my absent-mindedness have reached legendary proportions. The more anyone talks to my relatives, the more trivial details they get about my brain-scattered behaviour.

I left the car keys in the freezer compartment of the refrigerator, and tried to ignite the cooking gas with a ballpoint pen. I found my sunglasses half buried in the potted plant, walked into a party with one white and another grey pearl earring, and returned a library book with my flight tickets inside it.

I have attempted to open hotel rooms with my credit card, thrown the puppy with the bath water, applied shaving foam on my toothbrush, washed my hair with insect repellent and so on and so forth. The list is exhaustive.

My reading glasses have also had quite an adventurous journey. I have rescued them from the bottom of a shopping trolley, behind the vegetable peel, hidden under the newspapers or next to my gardening gloves, on top of the trash bin, in the laundry cupboard, and once, inside the washing machine.

My friends have suggested I buy a cord thingie that is attached to the two sides of the frames, and allows the specs to hang around the neck when not in use.

But it corresponds so much with a mental image I have of octogenarians, that I would rather die than subject myself to it. As long as I hold on to vanity, I will never become a senior citizen. I hope.

Lost in thought and finally giving up on the fruitless search, I sit on my reading chair and hear a faint crack. Jumping up, I see the sorry spectacles, broken into two neat halves.

"A string in time saves nine," my daughter misquotes.

"A stich in time…" I correct her.

"Glue to the rescue?" she prompts.

"Right! Wonderful clue," I agree.

Wedding Knot

Marriages are made in heaven, true.

But married lives are lived in Earth, with our feet planted firmly on terra firma. How do I know that? Let us just say I have experience, close to three decades of it, in this particular field.

So does that make me an expert on everything matrimonial? No, of course not. There is nothing static about a marital state, other than the wedding band. In this ever evolving and dynamic relationship, no set theories work, which is what I tell the hopeful unmarried youngsters who come to me for suggestions. On how to find the right partner and stay happily married, that is.

Over the years, some things have definitely changed. When my grandmother was asked what was the one quality she desired in a husband, she said she wanted to marry a man who wore long pants. I remember as a child, I would get ticked every time she related this tidbit to me. I could not believe her naiveté and between giggles would keep quizzing her. All the young men in her native village donned pajamas or other kinds of traditional clothing. But she was adamant about marrying someone who was suited-booted. And she did. My grandfather wore everything from tuxedoes to jodhpurs but I never spotted him in any Indian dress. Ever!

Was their marriage happy? I can't say, because I rarely saw them together. She was mostly indoors, cooking in the kitchen or knitting in the covered balcony. And he was always outdoors, zipping around in his fancy car or struggling with the plants in his

lawn. She would pull a thin veil over her head when she heard his footsteps approaching us. It left her face exposed but other than handing him tea, coffee or whatever the appropriate food item was, according to the time of the day, I never heard them even speak to one another.

My parents, on the other hand, could not stop talking to each other. It was their constant chatter that woke me up in the mornings, and also lulled me to sleep at night. My father met my mum's brother when they were journeying together on a train. They struck up a friendship and my Uncle invited my father to his house for dinner. My dad was travelling further up, but he impulsively decided to accept the invite. That evening he met my mom, and the rest was history.

The sequence of events describing what happened that fateful night would change, depending on whom you asked. Each of us children knew it by heart but we liked listening to it anyway. Were they happily wedded? Yes, of course.

I encountered my husband quite by chance too. Random terrorist activity had invited army intervention in the city where I studied, and my University was closed down for an indefinite time period. We were requested to go home. My spouse was doing a summer internship in the same town where my folks were posted.

Two days after I met him, he asked me what I was doing for the next seventy to eighty years. I said I was not sure, he said, will you marry me?

"What would you have done if I said no?" I inquired recently.

"Asked you again, with an offer you could never refuse," he announced.

"Like what?" I was curious.

"To become my laughing partner for one hundred years," he declared.

"Haha," I laughed

"Haha," he laughed back.

Mother of Mine

Battling illness is tough, especially the common 'flu'. That is because the viruses are so strong and varied that influenza has now become very difficult to overcome in the usual seven days or one-week period.

There was a time in my life when this infection was not even taken seriously. The nuns in my convent school, when presented with a medical letter of excuse explaining the sickness, frowned in disapproval. Sore throat and snivelling nose was not reason enough to avoid classes. A couple of sneezes here or there, and a slight fever meant you could skip the PE lesson, but that was all.

However, in a household bustling with siblings, it was a wonderful experience when the thermometer showed a rise in bodily temperature.

All parental attention suddenly centered on the unhealthy kid. It signaled the end of grappling with the hateful homework. It meant putting your feet up, and having your mother pamper you endlessly. It also indicated that you now had a priority over your brothers and sisters. All their comics and board games were handed to you, and the patient was allowed to win, without a fight.

I was a thin and delicate child, I am told. Fussy with food, I was partial to soups and juices where not much chewing had to be done. In the normal course, my no-nonsense mommy would not have any of it. I had to eat with the family and I had to swallow whatever was dished on my plate.

To the utter irritation of my older brother, I would carry on sitting in my dinning chair, conscientiously munching, long after everybody had finished eating. Once done, I would show him my polished platter, the state of which had to be dutifully reported to our mother.

Some days I would just about finish this entire laborious process when I would be called back for the next meal. There was no respite from it, unless some gluttonous cousins were visiting. I could then surreptitiously pass my food onto their bowl, whenever our hawkeyed mum was distracted.

Now that I look back, I don't think I managed to fool her entirely, because rather than argue over my suspiciously empty plate, she would make me drink up an extra tall glass of milk.

But ah! How my mother changed whenever I was down with fever. Her voice became gentle, her hand on my brow was cool, and while she propped me up to put spoonsful of broth into my mouth, a smile never left her tired face.

My father would also move his tea table to my room for the entire duration of my sickness. From behind a newspaper, he would continue to issue instructions for my well-being.

But it was always my mum I reached for in my delirium, and it was only her touch that could calm me down.

Last week, I suffered from a debilitating attack of the flu. Burning with fever, I was craving for my Ma. Having lost her more than a decade ago, I tried to bottle up my longing.

"Have the chicken soup please," a soft voice encouraged me.

"I don't feel like it," I said.

"What do you want Mom?" asked my daughter.

"I want my mother," I muttered, blinking back tears.

"I will be your mother," my spouse smiled.

"I will be your mother," our daughter chorused.

Spoiled for choice.

Holy Visitation

It was never going to be an easy experience.

Getting to meet Pope Francis on his gruelling Holy Land trip, that is. The International stadium in Amman was packed to capacity as I jostled with thousands of the gathered faithful at one of the many entrances.

The sunlight was bright and unrelenting, and tempers were threatening to rise with the rising temperatures. But the volunteers, handing complimentary water bottles and peak caps, helped to calm my nerves. Once inside the lavish grounds, a carnival scenario awaited us.

A stage was erected at one end of the field with two huge screens on either side, where live video recordings could be played. Young school children, in white uniform, walked with their teachers who were issuing smiling instructions at them.

All around, one could see families with infants in strollers. The remarkable thing was that the babies were not crying, but sleeping peacefully, oblivious to the din surrounding them.

The hymns, echoing from the loudspeakers, were in Arabic, welcoming the Pope to Amman. The lyrics were easy to follow and within moments, I joined in with the clapping and singing. It was sharp noon, and the gentle breeze was cool in the shade. Yet, under the scorching sun, my face was turning into a dark shade of tomato, and my skin was baking browner by the minute.

But these were small discomforts. Pope Francis was 77 years old at the time and had only one fully functioning lung. He had

battled influenza and fatigue, which had forced him to cancel some recent appointments to make an appearance here. Sunburn could not deter me.

Besides, if rank newborns could handle the heat, who was I to complain?

Suddenly, a mass of gigantic balloons appeared at various spots in the large arena. Pink, blue and white, they trailed one after the other into the sky. A drone of helicopters, signifying aerial security-watch, followed this.

Before I could understand what was going-on, an enthusiastic helper handed me a huge Jordanian flag and asked me to wave it. I was more than happy to pass off for a local. Balancing my parasol and a waving flag was a bit of a challenge, but I managed it.

White doves, that are a universal symbol of peace, were released from a podium. The crowd turned away from the stage as from the opposite direction, and an enormous truck made its appearance.

Standing upright in this roof-less mobile vehicle, the Pope embraced small children that were handed to him by their eager parents. The slow procession, lined by a crowd on both sides, made its way gradually to the raised platform.

Soon, the open air mass started. He spoke about putting aside everyone's grievances and divisions for the sake of unity. Peace was not something that could be bought but it was a gift to be crafted by our daily actions.

There must have been some magic in his sermon. On the way back, the same guards who were yelling at us in anger earlier smilingly opened the exit gates.

"Your face is so red!" one security policeman exclaimed.

"Yes," I agreed.

"You got sun burned?" he asked.

"Yes," I repeated.

"Ah, tomorrow the skin will peel off," he warned.

"But till then, I will radiate a holy glow," I smiled.

Understanding Accents

English is a universal language, spoken across the length and breadth of the globe.

All of us have our own versions of the Queen's English, but some of the accents the different communities use are likely to put the Imperial Monarch in a royal dilemma.

Kim Wong, a friend of mine, likes to record messages in my answering machine. He assumes that I can recognise his voice, because he never leaves his name with the message. His accent is distinctive, but it is impossible to decipher what he says. At least the first time round. But after several rewinds of the tape, I can just about manage to get a gist of the information that he has painstakingly left.

Returning Kim's call gets me invited to one more of his exhibitions at the Chinese arts and crafts store. Or he insists that I go to look at some exquisite pieces of artwork he has found. It is always most imperative that I visit that day itself.

Giving in to his persuasion, I find myself in the familiar surroundings of his brightly lit shop. As always, Kim is busy. With the headphones of an iPod stuck into his ears, he is singing along, loudly. I have to call out to him a couple of times before he even registers my presence.

Bowing to me profusely, he orders some Chinese tea.

"*Wercome, wercome,*" Kim greets me, his tongue uncomfortable with the '*l*' sound.

"Did you notice the cups? Made in occupied Japan in the time of the *Worrd Wall*," he enlightens me, pointing to a hand painted engraving at the bottom of the dainty teacups.

"World War," I correct him.

"Yes, yes, the tea should be sipped *velly srowry* to enjoy the taste, see?" he demonstrates, making a loud slurping sound.

"Very slowly," I repeat, but he loses interest in my corrections.

Born in Shanghai, he was fascinated with all kinds of hand-crafted items from a very early age. After working in Bangkok for the last few years, he decided to travel the world.

He speaks English with a strong Chinese accent and finds it almost impossible to pronounce certain alphabets. The '*l*' and '*r*' syllables cause him considerable grief, because he keeps interchanging them. Try as he might, even if he talks slowly, as if to a child, he can never manage it. Not in the first attempt anyway.

"This design was made in the *Ring* Dynasty," he tells me, pointing towards a graceful urn.

"What?" I look confused.

"Ling Dynasty," he states, shutting his eyes to focus on the right pronunciation.

"Of course," I nod in approval.

"You *wirr* buy it?" he asks.

"I don't know what I will do," I murmur, undecided.

"I *wirr* check with my boss and get you *speciarplice*," he says.

"Special price? Best discount?" I probe.

"I *wirr reave* a message *fol* you," he smiles.

"'Oh no," I exclaim.

"In your *answeling* machine," he twinkles.

Breath of Fresh Air

It is all about breathing, actually.

One takes some time to realise this, but that is all there is to it. With each cycle of inhaling and exhaling, we reinforce the fact that we are living beings. And the moment we stop breathing, we cease to be, in every sense of the term.

The very first gulp of air is forced into our tiny lungs the moment we are born. It is sometimes instigated by a smart slap on our behinds, by the obstetrician or mid-wife in charge.

Only after we yell back in response is a confirmation of our existence marked on our birth certificate. Subsequently, with every breath we take, our bodies grow and develop till we achieve adulthood. And finally, our last gasp transports us into an oblivion, from whence nobody has come back to tell the tale.

We are, of course, all familiar with this process. What comes as a big surprise is when the term *breathing,* is associated with inanimate things, like wine, and, particularly, red wine.

Most of us know nowadays which wines we like, but are still made to feel insufficient when we are in the company of a wine snob.

Who is that? I will tell you. It is easy to spot them in any party. They usually are the ones preaching about the wine, its year, the correct pronunciation, its maturity, the right temperature it should be stored at, the method in which to make it swirl, the cut of the glass in which it is served, and so on.

And all this is before they even get down to the 'decanting' part, which is a process of transferring the contents of a wine bottle into a wide bottomed, narrow necked decanter for sometime. So that it can *breathe*.

Wines which have been allowed to breathe, and therefore been aerated, give out more of an aroma and flavour upon serving. Such is the belief. And for the wine snob, it is also the gospel truth.

I am not an expert, and every glass of wine tastes pretty much the same to me. In fact, to be honest, it is by the intensity of the hangover that I suffer the next day that I conclude whether the wine served to me was of good quality, or not.

Not surprisingly, then, wine snobs tend to keep away from me. But the other night, at a party, I came across one, quite unexpectedly.

"This wine needs to breathe," a posh voice said.

"It has a nose?" I asked.

"You cannot decipher the wispy notes of lively rose and vanilla?" the accented voice countered.

"Nope, only the taste of fermented and dead grapes," I said.

"Should have been decanted for another hour," the voice insisted, ignoring me.

"Yes, or poured into a new bottle," I suggested, swivelling my glass.

One shapely eyebrow was arched at me in sarcasm, and the next instance, I was left alone.

I immediately breathed a sigh of relief.

A Rainy Interlude

In *My Fair Lady*, Eliza Doolittle sings, quite expansively, 'the rain in Spain stays mainly in the plain'.

If you remember the movie, it is Professor Higgins who makes her enunciate this in a speech exercise he designs to break her Cockney accent.

Audrey Hepburn, the coarse mouthed flower seller Eliza, and Rex Harrison, the arrogant phonetics instructor Henry Higgins, immortalised Bernard Shaw's characters from *Pygmalion*.

This little bit of literary trivia is pure nostalgia. It has no connection to the rain-lashings I experienced in the last fortnight. I was, of course, not in Spain, but in my home country India. The raindrops had assumed gigantic proportions and had turned into a torrential downpour.

The rainy season was not restricted to the metropolitan cities. Small towns, tiny villages, the hills and valleys, every inch of Indian soil was water drenched, and soaking wet. There were puddles everywhere. I had not seen a place so watery in a long while.

"I hope Indian homes have lightening conductors," said the voice in my head.

Thoughts of painful electrocution dampened my lunatic impulse of dancing in the rain. The sturdy umbrella was an absolute necessity, and my handbag bulged with hand-towels.

Drastic situations required such actions, you see.

Dainty stilettos were banished, as flat, rubber soled shoes

became my regular footwear. Within days I became an expert at figuring out which houses had a clothes-dryer versus those that made do with a clothesline. I could literally smell out the damp fungus.

A big rambling vehicle was hired as my car of choice. I also studiously memorised the timings when it was suicidal to be on Delhi roads.

Despite all the precautions, I was stuck for extended hours in incessant traffic jams. I learned how to make long and useless conversations on the cell phone. With the mobile talk-time in India, possibly the cheapest in the world, I swapped food recipes and life histories with all my casual acquaintances.

I became an avid follower of the FM car-radio, and fidgeted with the audio settings. Every few seconds I switched channels, much to the annoyance of the other passengers.

Delhi, an ancient sprawling city, got a freshly washed look after the heavy rains. The foliage developed a bloom, and there was verdant greenery everywhere. Its claim of being the greenest city in Asia acquired a tinge of truthfulness. The vast parks and lush trees became visible once the grime was rinsed off.

By the end of my holiday I became immune to the relentless rain, but all the slush made me wistful for a bit of sunshine. I could not wait to get back to Amman.

Emerging from the airport in Jordan I looked heavenwards and heaved a sigh of relief. But as I rolled my luggage trolley towards the car park, the sky became dark suddenly, and it started raining.

"You brought this rain with you," my husband said accusingly.

"I bought the umbrellas too," I said.

"Where are they?" asked spouse.

"Somewhere over the rainbow," I sang.

"Raindrops are falling on my head," he complained.

"Let's get into the car instead," I joked.

Birth Pangs

I have always looked forward to the turn of the year.

As the twelve months of the Gregorian calendar complete their annual run, and the diary runs out of pages, it is time to usher in new beginnings.

January has a sparkle associated with it. It is named after Janus, the Roman God of the doorway. He is depicted with two faces: one gazing at the past, and the other looking into the future.

I was born in this month.

But I had to share it with one of my siblings, who appeared a few years before me, also in January. Yet, since in a family of five, these were the only two birthdays in a common month, it was given exceptional status.

My brother thought it was because of his thrilling arrival, while I was convinced it was because of my angelic one. Throughout our childhood, we were unable to resolve this prickly issue.

I am told that as a child, I did not like to get my feet dirty. A tiny speck of dirt was enough to bother me. Even after a fierce quarrel, when in the heat of the moment I had flung my shoes at my brother, he still had to carry me.

I would keep sitting on a chair unless some slippers were provided, or demand to be piggybacked. Now that I think of it, my heart goes out to that young boy who carried his sulking sister on his bony shoulders.

He was the chief protector of my party frock also. What is a party frock?

When I was growing up, my sensible mother made me wear my older sibling's hand-me-downs. My school hours stretched throughout the day, where I was attired in a ghastly uniform. When I got back to the house, I was made to change into home clothes. These were identical for my brothers and me, consisting of shorts and t-shirts with an occasional sweater in the winter months.

The only concession made for me was the solitary party frock that my mom hand-stitched. It had ruffles, frills, bows and sashes, and looked like a fairy dress.

My brothers and I were filled in awe, just by looking at it. It would hang prominently in my cupboard, among the other shabby clothes until, on very important occasions, I was allowed to wear it.

There would be immediate requests for me to twirl around in front of my family. My mother issued strict instructions to my brother, who was assigned the thankless task of protecting it from any spill, tear or ruin.

So from dusting the chair I was sitting on, to tucking a bib around my throat when I ate ice cream or candy, my brother would do his duty.

I always wanted to ask him, why he did not refuse. Recently, when we were together on my birthday I finally cornered him.

"How could you be so nice to me when we were children?" I questioned, before blowing the candles on the cake.

"I am still nice to you, and please don't get the icing on your dress," my brother cautioned.

"Why not?" I countered.

"Ok, go ahead," he said wrapping a protective napkin around my neck.

"Mum would be proud of you," I assured him.

"I am proud of you," he reassured me.

The Legend and I

When a legend dies, there is a pall of gloom that descends all over the world.

If the deceased person has lived for close to a century, twenty-seven of those years in prison, and after release, served one term as President of his country, his stature assumes epic proportions.

To form any connection with such a dignitary is an ambitious and formidable task. But reading the obituaries and accolades that were pouring forth after his demise, I remembered my own fleeting association with him.

I first heard about Nelson Rolihlahla Mandela when I reviewed his autobiographical book *Long Walk to Freedom*.

Actually that is not true. Several months before the book was launched, and he went on to become the first democratically elected President of South Africa, I was asked to interview him. He was passing through Abu Dhabi. The year was 1993 and he had recently been freed from his long captivity in Robben Island.

I was very excited to be meeting such a noble statesman in real life. But to my utter dismay, by the time I reached the hotel where he was staying he had already checked out. There was some bungle up with the timing, and the general manager kept apologising profusely to me.

Seeing my crestfallen expression, he offered to make arrangements to have me meet the people who had come in contact with him. The most interesting of them was the iron man.

It so happened that when Nelson Mandela was putting on his trademark colourful shirt that morning, he found that it was ironed to perfection. In his customary manner, he wanted to personally thank the person who had pressed it so immaculately. The housekeeping staff was summoned, who was in turn asked to call the expert with the steam iron.

Mandela, however, in his usual way, insisted that he should be taken to the servant's quarters, rather than the launderer be brought to his suite.

Thus he was escorted to the back of the hotel, through the staff elevator, to the room where the laundry man was ironing clothes.

Seeing an entire delegation at his door without warning, the poor worker almost collapsed in nervousness. But completely unfazed, Mandela expressed his gratitude in person, shook him by the hand, and told him what a great job he had done.

Soon, I moved to South Africa on a transfer. It was 1997 and the whole of Johannesburg was in a romantic mood. Their President was in love with Graca Machel and was wooing her relentlessly.

Mandela was seventy-nine and she was fifty-one. Along with everyone else, I started calling him *Madiba*, meaning grandfather. The President, despite his retinue of bodyguards, was relishing his freedom and would turn up everywhere.

One day I was in a shopping mall. I heard a bit of commotion and turned around to see Mandela carefully picking long-stemmed red roses. There was already a box of chocolates in his hand.

"Sweets for your sweet and flowers for your honey?" I asked, waving at him frantically.

The legend stopped, and smiled. And quite unexpectedly, he ruffled my hair.

When I read about his passing away recently, all that I could recall was the warm touch of his hand on my head.

Snow Diary

I knew it snowed in Amman.

I had seen pictures of snow covered houses and streets even before I relocated to the city. But somehow, because of my hectic travel schedule that took me away from the country, I always missed witnessing the snowfall.

When I got back, I would be told stories about it. How thick the white carpet was over the grass, buildings and the trees, turning random undulating roads into instant ski slopes. Once I returned from a trip to find residual bits of snow in some remote areas of town too.

But what I wanted was to be bang in the midst of it.

Jordanians pray for heavy rains because that is the easiest way to irrigate their water-deprived land. Most of the rainfall here, takes place in the winter months. So, along with the locals, I was sending out my prayers to the Good Lord too. But I was going a step forward in my fervent entreaties, and asking for the raindrops to become frozen, and float down as snowfall.

I began to study the weather columns regularly, even though I was aware that what the weathermen predicted had little or no resemblance to what the conditions actually turned out to be.

This was especially true if you were visiting London, and staying in a hotel there. The housekeeping staff supplied a card, with the forecast temperatures of the next day, pinned to your pillow. Daily. It was a thoughtful gesture, designed to help the guests dress themselves up appropriately in warm or cool clothes.

But the problem was that the predicted weather report was always erroneous. I had, on several occasions, left my umbrella in the room, having taken the advice on the pillow, and got caught in thundershowers. Or, expecting a heavy downpour, lugged it around the entire day, only to have the sun beaming at me from a cloudless sky.

Anyway, despite my long experience of incorrect forecasts, last week I scanned every weather report there was to read. All of them said snowfall was expected in Amman the next day.

I canceled all my traveling plans immediately, and decided to stay put at home. I dragged my chair close to the bay window and positioned myself there. In my enthusiasm, I even pressed my nose too hard into the glass, leaving a sharp imprint. Everything was eerily quiet; it was still the early morning hours.

Just as I was about to give up, little wisps of curly white flakes came drifting down. It was magical. I slid the window open, and stretched my hand out. Within minutes I could catch some of it in my palm. I was ecstatic and could not stop smiling.

Snowfall is a noiseless activity. There is an uncanny silence all around, with the powdery white tendrils floating, like torn pieces of a cloud, which settle on the ground.

Unfortunately, the magic didn't last. After the fourth day of nonstop snowing, I got fed up. The TV was on static and the Internet was down. A thick mound of snow outside my front door made it difficult to open it. The romance that I associated with snowfall was fast fading.

In truth, I was beginning to feel claustrophobic. All my earlier prayers to the heavens above had been answered, so I was shamefaced about asking God to now halt the snowstorm.

With Christmas round the corner I searched for new benefactors.

And began praying, quite fervently, to Santa Claus.

New Year Resolution

Time and tide wait for no man.

But every now and then, it is worthwhile to examine how to manage our work life balance more beneficially.

All of us would ideally like to spend more hours with our loved one, for instance, but are unable to do so because of diverse constraints. We also want to have a healthy routine and plan it enthusiastically. But contingencies interrupt routine and disrupt it.

Therefore, we make New Year resolutions. It might seem like a childish activity and to me it did appear like one, for a long period. That is because the nuns in my school were the ones who coached me into this exercise. In their sombre manner, they encouraged me to write a list of things I would improve within myself, in the coming year.

They were very cunning, these Carmelite sisters. If I wrote *I would read more*, as one of the resolves, they wrote, *course books, not story books*, next to it.

Or, for instance, if I jotted down *I will go to bed on time*, I would find, *after saying your prayers*, written in red ink on top of the resolution.

Initially it was very interactive, this formulating of my New Year pact, you see. It was not just I, making an effort to make myself better, but the entire nun's brigade, which was there to uplift me. They helped me to become mentally strong, and made sure I got rid of all my bad habits.

This early training lasted into my college years too. Any rule that I accidentally broke within the first few weeks of the brand new year could be corrected immediately, by making a re-resolve to stick by it. I tried very hard, you see.

And then, for a period of time I stopped. I mean I did not stop making the list but I, kind of, re-cycled the same one. It generally began with, *I will start exercising*, followed somewhere down the line with *I will not eat junk food*, and always concluded with *I will call up my mother more often.*

After the tragic loss of my parents, I quit making New Year resolutions. "What was the point," said the voice in my head. My self-improvement was not going to get them back for me.

But that did not prevent me from finding out what other people were putting on their lists. It was fun to discover that, and at the first opportunity I would ask around.

Many would not be very forthcoming. But some had no such qualms, and would readily supply me with all the information.

At a college reunion recently, I met up with an ex-student who was several batches junior to me. A former advertising executive, he had branched into his own creative business now.

"My New Year resolution remains the same since 1986," he told me.

"And what is that?" I asked.

"To quit smoking," he confessed, flicking ash from his cigarette.

"It has obviously not worked," I observed.

"It is an uphill task but I am going to give it up. Mark my words," he assured me.

"Give up the smoking or the resolution?" I teased.

"One or the other," he resolved.

"Fair enough," I said, giving him the thumbs up.

Peaches and Cream

Sometimes the simplest thing can open a floodgate of memories.

Just recently, a basket of peaches was hand-delivered at my doorstep by a sweet neighbour of mine. The gesture was so sudden and unexpected that it took me a moment to recover from the surprise. And then I was suffused with utter delight.

The container was overloaded with the luscious fruit. I picked one up to peer at it closely. The colour of the swollen cheeks ranged from pale yellow to dark flushed red. I inhaled the heady fragrance, and was instantly transported to my grandfather's garden.

My mother's dad, who we called *Nana* in our Indian language, was a very strict man. Incidentally in Arabic, Nana is the term used for mint and for a long time I had trouble asking for mint-tea because I had to say *'Nana chai'* and the phrase would get stuck in my throat. His angry face swam in front of my eyes, and I would quickly switch my order, to a more harmless cup of coffee.

My grandpa was a perfectionist and retired from active employment at the age of fifty-eight. My grandmother said that was the prime of his youth, and he did not know what to do with his excessive store of physical energy.

So he started to apply himself to domestic matters with the same dedication that he had employed in his professional life. This meant that suddenly, stuff that ran smoothly beneath the benign and lenient gaze of my grandma became a stringent and regimented exercise under his command.

He began supervising everything-from following the cleaner

to see that each nook and cranny of a room was mopped up, instructing the launderer to focus on the upturned shirt collars, checking individual piece of fruit and vegetable that was passed into the kitchen, and making sure the cuts of meat were of superior variety.

To us, the hoards of children who were unceremoniously bundled into carriages and in later years into cars by our zealous mother and taken to our grandparents' house for the long summer vacation, this took the form of an annual nightmare. There were more rules in my grandfather's house than in my convent school.

And then he started working on his orchard. With wily precision he enticed all the kids to help him in this assignment. We had jobs in rotation: to water the garden, time the sprinklers, prune the buds or pick the fruit. To add more excitement, he introduced a small tip for the most enthusiastic fruit picker.

Peach season was the best. The trees would bend under the weight of the succulent fruit. The scented peaches that smelled of sweet nectar dazzled our senses. While eating it the juice trickled down, and give us sticky hands and cheeks. The glorious summer evenings resonated with peals of childish laughter, as we lolled about on the grass.

In a blind fit of nostalgia I picked up the phone and called my husband.

"I grow old, I grow old. I shall wear the bottom of my trousers rolled," I quoted.

"Hello?" said my spouse.

"Shall I part my hair behind? Do I dare to eat a peach?" I continued.

"Hello?" he repeated.

"I shall wear white flannel trousers, and walk upon the beach," I recited.

"Who is this?" he asked.

"TS Eliot," I supplied.

"Save some peaches and cream for me also Mr. Eliot," he laughed, slamming the phone down.

Rhyme and Reason

At the very outset, let me confess that I have nothing against babies.

I do like to admire them-from a safe distance. Given the right opportunity, I coo over them, pinch their cheeks and even cuddle them. The fact that very often the possessive mothers brush my hesitant overtures aside is another matter altogether.

But really, I do like babies. I don't have much in common with them, but I like the idea of liking them.

They look particularly adorable while sleeping, fists tightly clenched, eyes firmly shut and the eyelashes sweeping over the chubby cheeks. They all look angelic, and cherubic. Viewing them in this vulnerable state is like glimpsing a bit of divinity itself.

However, that is where my admiration of them begins and ends. Once they are awake and exercising the full power of their lungs, I want to just run away.

But I don't seem to be able to escape wailing babies. I can be anywhere: in an aircraft, watching a movie, taking a train/bus journey or in any public space with strangers, and a couple of piercing baby wails will, without fail, assail my eardrums.

I don't know how this happens. Maybe it is just heavenly providence.

Recently, I was taking a long haul non-stop flight. I wished fervently that I would not be placed next to a bawling baby. Someone heard my silent entreaty, and I found myself sharing a row with elderly people. Across the aisle, though, was a lady with a three-year-old child for company.

I have no quarrel with small toddlers, especially the talkative ones. I enjoy listening to their childish lisping voices.

I liked my little travel companion immediately because she was in a mood to recite poetry. Sitting up straight in her seat, she was meticulously going through all the nursery rhymes.

By the time I put my hand baggage on the overhead locker I had already heard a singsong recitation of: *Ba Ba Black Sheep* and *Twinkle Twinkle Little Star*.

Then she started narrating: *Pussy Cat, Pussy Cat, Where Have You Been*. Maybe her mother had told her where the flight was headed, because when the kid would reach the next line she would suddenly shriek: *I've Been To London, To look At The Queen*, and double up with laughter.

When the mirth subsided, she would go right back to the first line of the nonsense verse.

I tried to distract her with *Jack And Jill*, and *Piggy On The Rail Road*, but she would have none of it. Pussy Cat, Pussy Cat went on for the rest of the flight.

Several hours later I had the poem etched in my brain in permanent indelible ink. When we landed and lined up for immigration it was still playing in my head.

"Name please," asked the officer at the desk.

"Pussy cat," I said automatically without thinking.

"Really? Where have you been?" he asked in astonishment.

"Now in London to visit the queen," I answered.

"Ok, whatever else you do here, don't frighten the rats under the chair," he ordered, stamping my passport.

Coughing Up

If one considers all the involuntary sounds that come from one's throat, coughing is the worst.

Snoring incidentally, does not qualify in this category because that is done when one is sleeping, and in most cases the snorer does not quite agree to the fact that he, well, snores.

So, between sneezing, yawning and coughing, the three primary reflex actions that originate at the mouth, the last one is the most irritating-for both the individual who is suffering the attack, and the persons who are within a hearing distance of it.

Sneezing and yawning can be made soundless with a little practice, of course. One could, with some grit and determination, even swallow it. All you need to do is clamp your jaw, tightly. And that automatically gets rid of the problem.

But coughing is very tricky, and it is a different phenomenon altogether. When a bout of this body-racking spasm occurs, no amount of jaw clenching or nervous swallowing helps.

A cough usually accompanies fever and chest congestion but lingers on long after the earlier two have subsided. It's probably owing to this singular persistence that idiomatic usage such as *cough up the information* is associated with a forced delivery.

From babies to the elderly, everyone has suffered some experience or the other with coughing in its different variations: from the dry bronchial cough, to the eardrums shattering whooping cough.

However, the best of all is a situation generated artificial cough. What is that? Also called imitation cough, this is something that a cougher supplies instinctively, according to the demands of a situation.

It is generally used as a warning sound, by a partner in crime, about the arrival of an authoritarian figure. It is learnt in early childhood, and it is a great way to cover up for all the mischief that one is accused of doing.

In more conservative families, where the ladies kept themselves traditionally veiled, the gentlemen were taught to announce their arrival with a discrete cough. It gave a chance to the women to get into their conventional attire, if they so desired, and avoid any social awkwardness.

I had an older cousin who had the unlikely distinction of creating a *mock coughing code*. All the younger siblings, including me, had to follow the drill every time we met up during the long summer vacations in our ancestral home.

One short cough meant the ice candy man was approaching. Two bark-like coughs signaled the appearance of our adored uncle, who took us to the circus and ferry rides. For stealing mangoes or guavas from a neighbourhood tree, there was a succession of coughs to be tracked.

I thought I had forgotten the encryption of the *MCC*.

My last bout of flu had left me with a lingering sore throat, but I was in for a surprise as soon as my phone rang.

"Guess who?" asked the voice on the phone.

"Cough!" is all that I could manage.

"You eating ice-cream in this state?" the voice scolded.

"Cough, Cough," I responded.

"Uncle Dan is visiting you?" she queried.

"Cough, Cough, Cough," I coughed.

"Did you steal some apples too?" she laughed.

"My Coughing Cousin!" I shrieked in delight, before dissolving into a bout of coughs.

Holiday Burden

Every time the festive season is upon us, the residents of Amman have to gear up for an unpleasant time.

We are blessed with cooler weather, compared to the neighbouring countries that swelter in the heat, so Jordan experiences an onslaught of visitors that is quite unprecedented.

Being the perfect host is difficult, when the guests are so ill mannered. Flouting all traffic rules, they congregate on the roundabouts, park in no-parking areas, occupy noisy tables in restaurants, and leave heaps of rubbish trailing after them.

It is a good idea to pack your bags and head out of the city for this duration. But sometimes one is stuck, because family or friends decide to honour you with their presence. And then one's goose is truly and completely cooked.

My parents taught me that house guests were a version of divinity itself and I must treat them with great respect and provide them all the creature comforts.

In India, there is an ancient saying in Sanskrit, which roughly translated means, 'guest is God!'

During my childhood I saw that my mother saved the finest cutlery, crockery, bed linen, towel sets et al, for the visitors. Even my grandfather, who was unusually stern and bad tempered and quite unlike how a loving grandparent should be, kept the best room of his huge mansion locked up.

It was supposed to be for *VIPs* and, till today, I have only managed to peep into that room once. It had a huge four-poster bed, a wooden fireplace, and lace curtains, but I could not explore further, because I heard a warning cough by my vigilant cousin. It announced the arrival of my irate grandpa, and I fled from the scene before my ears could be boxed.

In the olden days, even though families were large, there was an unwritten rule, which everyone followed. For instance, the visitors lent a hand in everything. So when my mom cooked, the other visiting ladies chopped the vegetables. If the domestic help were fixing the extra beds, some uncle took it upon himself to supervise the arrangements.

But somewhere along the way things changed. Societies became more self-centred and the worst affected were the relatives. Both ungrateful and selfish, their demands overrode any sense of propriety. No amount of generous hospitality was good enough for them.

To counter this, I started collecting brochures, several hundreds of them. From restaurants, beauty parlours, car hire companies, tourist attractions to yellow pages and Turkish bath sites, I had them all.

When a particularly grumpy relative visited us with his entire clan, I put them at his bedside.

Next morning presented a typical scene.

"I was pressing this call-bell. Why did the maid not respond?" he said to me belligerently.

"What do you want?" I asked.

"Some fresh pancakes should be sent up to my room immediately," he ordered.

"Why didn't you eat it at breakfast?" I inquired.

"I did not feel like at the time. I want to have some now, is that a problem?" he glared at me.

"It is the lunch hour, why don't you have it tomorrow?" I reasoned.

"Now, I want it now!" he insisted, regressing from age forty, to age four.

That is precisely when I handed him the hotel pamphlet, before marching him out.

Memory Tales

When my daughter was a toddler, her favourite hobby was listening to stories.

More than having fairy tales read out to her, what she preferred was, a glimpse into my own past. She longed to know everything about me as a child, and her most persistent plea used to be 'your story Mom, please'.

A promise of that retelling would get her charged up. She would complete her nightly rituals in double quick time. Dinner swallowed, teeth brushed, bath finished and hair combed, she would present herself like a sweet little angel.

She would insist I lie next to her in the turned down bed. Clasping my wrist tightly in her little hand, she would stare dreamily into space before making her selection.

Like a story book has chapters, she had divided my early years into similar sections. So, the decision to make her mom aged three, four, or five depended on her. For some reason, she never ventured further from these three ages. And now that I think about it, I also never inquired why it was this specific part of my infancy that fascinated her the most.

But she listened with rapt attention, sometimes forgetting to even blink.

The first five to ten minutes were spent in a warm-up, which was usually like a prologue. She would say, for instance, 'Mommy, today I want to hear the story of when you were four and went to

that picnic in a bus'. When I tried to feign forgetfulness, she would start off the tale in her childish treble, word for word.

She was a smart child and never allowed me to take poetic liberties. So, if I flung a bottle of orange juice at someone in a particular story, it could not become apple juice in the next narration. A sharp reprimand of 'silly Mummy' would greet me if I ever made even the minutest change to the script. I had to acknowledge the mistake, and make immediate amends.

This daily mental exercise kept my memory in a razor sharp condition. At the drop of a hat I could recreate my past life for the delightful entertainment of my little one.

But her most favourite story was of her mom aged four.

This was when I had taken part in a fancy-dress competition. One neighbourhood Aunt had decked me as a child bride. Her own son, a thin and scrawny chap, was dressed up as my bridegroom.

In all my bridal finery when I marched confidently onto the stage, I was instantly awarded the first prize. But being one half of a team, I had to share it with my groom.

What I got was a seashell keychain, but what my teammate received was a beautiful long pencil. It also had a back-scratching attachment connected to it.

It was exactly at this point of the story telling that my daughter would start screeching with laughter.

"So, what did you do Mom?" she would ask, fully knowing the expected answer.

"I snatched the pencil from the boy and told him if he cried I would give him something to collect his tears in," I would thunder.

This made her jump on the bed in excitement.

"I know Mom, because a cry baby's best friend is?" she would leave the question hanging.

"A bucket!" we would chorus, to the clapping of her hands.

Silent Benefits

As I grow older, I find there are days when I don't feel like talking.

To anyone and everyone, that is. For a previous chatterbox, this is a strange thing to happen, and I am still trying to understand the implications of it. Maybe it has something to do with my childhood.

The maximum number of punishments I suffered from the disciplinary nuns who raised me, were for talking. Oh how much I was reprimanded in school. There was one particular month I remember, where I spent more time outside the classroom, than inside it.

Our classes had two doors, one in the front side and one at the back. The ever-vigilant sisters tiptoed from either of the two doorways to catch me in the act. They would point at a poster saying *silence please,* in front of which I would be found chattering, and march me off to stand in complete solitude, outside the class.

I spoke out of turn and I spoke my mind. I spoke up and I spoke down. In other words, once I found my voice, it became very difficult to hush me. My teachers would say *empty vessels make the most sound* in an idiomatically cryptic way that they had of imparting knowledge. But for me it was *water off a duck's back,* another idiom that they drilled into us.

It was not entirely my fault you see. The thoughts whizzing in my head were so many that I could hardly find the time to voice them all in any normal day. It is no wonder that I sometimes talked even in my sleep. Mumbled and incoherent words, but I spoke them nevertheless.

When I was passing out of school, my headmistress wrote, *think before you speak* in my farewell note, instead of the usual *best wishes in your future endeavours*. I guess she reasoned that I would never abandon talking, so it was better to caution me on the safety aspects of free speech, rather than ask me to give it up altogether.

I did not pay much heed to this suggestion. The result was that during my own wedding ceremony I had to be scolded by the priest for interrupting him.

I wanted the mantras to be explained to me in simple language, instead of the complex Sanskrit, so that I could understand the promises I was making to my bridegroom, before I made them.

The pundit enlightened me, of course he did. But we got into a sort of philosophical discussion, which made him miss his next assignment and for which he never forgave me.

Somewhere along the way I found that resting my vocal chords gave me greater peace, than exercising them. And I learned more by listening, than talking.

I could, with a gesture of my eye or hand, steer a conversation towards any direction. Without uttering a single syllable.

The other day I tried it, one more time.

"Politeness and chivalry is dead I tell you, completely redundant. Everyone skips the queue, absolutely everyone," complained a suave aristocratic looking gent, sitting on the last seat of a transit bus that was driving us to the airplane.

I was standing, and when he looked at me, I just raised one eyebrow.

There was a split second pause.

"Ah! Please sit here. I totally insist," said the gentleman, jumping up and grinning sheepishly, before launching into another tirade.

Benefits of silence?

Lipstick on Your Collar

Salespeople are becoming very aggressive, I tell you. They inundate you with messages, via texts and phone. It is impossible to evade the clutches of a telemarketer once you make the mistake of answering a few innocuous sounding queries.

Venturing forth into a shopping mall is like inviting unnecessary trouble. Especially from the makeshift booths, which some shops construct, in the middle of a walkway. These are located between the stores that line both sides of a mall, and have a glass counter, a few stools, and the most persistent marketers on the planet.

When I see them, I employ a strategy that I have perfected. I put my head down, like really sinking low into my torso sort of down, and walk with lengthy steps away from them. Alternately, in order to keep them from approaching me, I whip out my mobile phone and pretend to have an urgent discussion.

But still, once in a while I slip up. It happened last weekend and in that split second that my concentration wavered, I was cornered. A man who was holding a few make-up products inquired very casually, about the shade of lipstick that I was wearing. Just like that!

Nobody had ever asked me such a question before, least of all a stranger. He stood in front of me, waiting patiently for a reply as I struggled to come up with the right response.

The truth was that I did not remember. I had dressed up in a

rush, and had blindly smeared the first lipstick I could find in my dresser, onto my mouth.

Why had I done so? Mainly because in Amman, people are so fashionable that women wear pearls even to the vegetable market, so I felt that this was the least I could do towards making myself look presentable.

But I had definitely not memorised the colour of my lipstick.

So when he asked me if he could show me some latest arrivals, which might suit my skin tone, I could not think of an immediate rebuff. The minute I neared the counter, I heard *Lipstick on Your Collar* song blaring from the speakers.

Inviting me to sit on a high chair, he offered to give a free make-up demonstration. Like a canvas painter, he took out several brushes and tubes of lipstick and started working on my face. In a few minutes, a small crowd had gathered around us.

With deft strokes he applied the colours, all the while giving a running commentary. I was told that early Mesopotamian women were the first ones to crush gemstones and use them as lipstick.

Also, I was informed that initially in England, only upper class women and male actors wore makeup. Generally men considered women wearing lipstick as more feminine, than those who do not, he added.

"Your shade is burnt tangerine, and you must wear it all the time," he announced eventually.

I peered at my mouth, which he had outlined in a cupid's bow.

It looked alien and puffed up in a pout.

"The silicon oil in our brand of lipstick seals the colours, so it will never leave a mark on your teacup," he recited the sales pitch.

"But it will make a hole in my pocket," I complained.

"You are worth it. Imagine, no lipstick on his collar," he said, presenting me with the bill.

Green-eyed Monster

Have you ever wondered why jealousy is called a green-eyed monster?

Also, why is it that people turn green with envy? Green is supposed to be a vibrant colour so how come it is associated with something sinister? Should it not convey wholesomeness and positivity?

Especially, since green leafy vegetables are life sustaining. Moreover, the verdant trees and foliage supply us with endless quantities of oxygen that is vital to human existence.

When I was a child, it was the easiest thing in the world to frighten me. My siblings, both boys, should have made me immune to the presence of snails, caterpillars and squiggly earth worms appearing between the pages of my school books. But it didn't and I would get scared every time a practical joke was played on me.

If a frog jumped at me from my shoe rack, followed by devilish laughter from my brothers' room, I would go barefoot for the next few days and not venture anywhere near the shelf.

My ribbons would disappear, and scented erasers were chewed up regularly.

But what was most disturbing in all this was the green-eyed monster the boys claimed was guilty of all this. He supposedly had a bulging forehead, buck teeth, web-like hands, and dark green eyes without lashes. Also, he never blinked but stared, well, unblinkingly.

One mention of him would have me agreeing to do all sorts of menial tasks, like carrying their school bags or completing their homework.

Long before I read Shakespeare's description of jealousy, as a green-eyed monster in *Othello*, I had already made my acquaintance with it as a child. Sibling rivalry had taught me a lot.

So, at any costume party, I would never agree to become a monster. I was a Pumpkin, Nurse, Urchin, Cinderella, Snow-white, Red Riding Hood, and once I even went disguised as a Book, with pages and all (my mom's ingenuity was legendary).

But a monster, green eyed one, even with a chance in a million to be allowed to buy fancy contact lenses? Never!

Last week my husband handed me a bunch of party invites. I was given the job of selecting which ones we wanted to attend. There was an upcoming masquerade ball that sounded interesting. We sent in our acceptance.

A day before the event, I woke up to suddenly find my left eye bathed in a reddish hue. There was no pain or irritation but I had burst a tiny blood vessel in my conjunctiva, which is the white part of the eye.

"I think I should go as a pirate with an eye patch," I told my spouse.

"Why don't you remove the patch and go as your normal self?" he smirked.

"But I look like a monster," I was horrified.

"Yes, a red eyed one," he agreed

I bared my teeth at him, before stomping off.

"Listen! It is any day better than the green eyed one," he announced, to my retreating back.

Baby in Pink

There is hardly any person in the world that does not like babies. You know those cuddly warm bundles that smell of powder and sunshine. They have an uncanny ability to cut across all barriers of race or ethnicity, and when a mischievous infant beams at you, it is impossible not to respond to its toothy grin.

But as mankind becomes increasingly intolerant towards each other, it is no longer acceptable to admire kids that are strangers to you. Parents are paranoid about their children. Forget about offering a candy or a rattle to a child, even smiling at them impulsively invites a frown from their over protective minder.

This is just my observation, but it doesn't bother me at all. I do not smile at these little people too much anyway. In fact given half a chance I make faces at them, from a safe distance, of course.

Why so? That is because I seem to attract babies. It is as if I have an invisible in-built magnet that pulls them towards me. The more I try to avoid them the more they follow me around.

I can be anywhere and minding my own business, when they appear out of thin air to bother me. Toddlers find their way towards me the moment they are set on the floor, and this happens not once or twice, but every irritating time.

God alone knows why they have made it their chosen mission to target a harmless person, but that's just the way it is. They go to extreme lengths to catch my attention, like offering me their soother,

waddling up to push my handbag, reaching out to pull my reading glasses, and so on and so forth.

The more persistent types lift their little arms and demand to be picked up, and the ones who know my name, lisp loudly, and ask me to drop everything I am doing, to listen to them.

I used to make funny faces to scare them away. Like rolling my eyes, puffing my cheeks, or, when the parents were not looking, sticking my tongue out.

But even that is not working in my favour these days, because the little rascals think it is some kind of a game, and giggle hysterically.

When I look at the baby pictures of our daughter, I am swamped with memories.

The preferred colour of her infancy was pink.

It was strange because other than falling into this stereotype I did not raise her like a typical girl whose only role in life is to switch from being someone's daughter to becoming somebody's wife. Coming from a country where female children are treated as unwanted baggage, I tried my best to inculcate confidence, responsibility and self-belief in her.

And yet, watching her completely engrossed in her professional life, I feel nostalgic for that baby in the pink pinafore.

She has long outgrown my lap, and towers over me, insisting that I have shrunk. But as a mother, along with all my love and blessings I have one more wish for her.

Despite my aversion for babies, I fervently hope that she retains her childlike curiosity and enthusiasm.

Forever!

All About a Sari

If I were to document the greatest compliments that I have ever received in my life, the best ones would be when I was seen and admired in a sari.

Why would I embark on such a seemingly vain exercise?

Well, it is the quickest way of raising yourself-esteem, in the shortest possible time. Without exception, it has made my day brighter, every time that I have tried it. Vanity aside, it is a magical mood enhancer.

In India, the sight of ladies wearing saris is a norm rather than a novelty. This is how it should be, considering it is our national dress. For the women, that is. It is popular among the females of the neighbouring countries too, though not universally, I must add. Other garments vie for attention.

Despite new fashionable clothes creeping into our social structure, irrespective of age or class, saris remains our most traditional outfit. There would hardly be any woman in my homeland that does not own at least one sari. This excludes small children of course, though little girls in some fishing villages also wear a smaller version of one.

So, what is a sari? For those unfamiliar with this costume, let me explain. It has two spellings, to begin with. You can call it either sari, or saree. It means one and the same thing, whether you extend the vowel at the end of the word or not.

Derived from ancient Sanskrit, sari is the name given to a long strip of unstitched cloth, which is between four to nine yards in length. It is wrapped around the body in a particular systematic manner. At a casual glance, it resembles a floor length gown.

But the million-dollar question is that if it is unstitched, how does it stay on the waist, and not collapse in a heap, at the feet of the wearer?

That is because the outfit has two other parts to it too. There is a blouse for the upper body that is short, leaving the midriff bare. Also, an underskirt, called a petticoat, is tied at the waist.

One extension of the Sari is tucked into it, while the other end goes over the left shoulder. At the middle, a set of pleats are arranged by folding the cloth to form, a sort of, compact fan shape. The entire ensemble gives the appearance of petals that are arranged very decoratively in a flower.

Most women wear their saris in this manner but there are more than fifty ways to drape it. In different parts of the country, according to their whim, the ladies alternate the loose end of the saree, over the left or the right shoulder.

Where I am concerned, I love saris and wear one at the slightest excuse. And I've noticed that the compliments keep flowing, fast and furious when I am dressed in one.

But in an alien country, it attracts a lot of attention from foreigners, and I keep getting asked the same questions, over and over again.

Recently, at a formal gathering I had to give an impromptu demonstration about the several parts of the garment, one more time.

"Beautiful! But can you tell me how it stays up, this unstitched piece of cloth?" asked an inquisitive voice.

I turned around to see a baldish man, leering at me.

"Oh that? We have to exercise every bit of will power, now if you excuse me I have to go and practise," I replied, before walking off.

Tumbling Fortunes

Over-enthusiastic hosts make me nervous.
I like casual get-togethers, with no pre-designed format, other than the seating arrangement.

I was not so particular about this when I was younger, but there were times when I was made to sit next to a large potted plant, or a swinging kitchen door. Once, my chair almost disappeared into the adjoining washroom. It was most uncomfortable, I must say. And so now I demand a decent dinner seat.

Given a choice between sitting down and eating, or wolfing down my food standing up, I prefer the former. So I am always grateful to be directed towards a chair, which has my nametag on it. There is no confusion and everyone, the hosts as well as the guest, is happy.

But I intensely dislike party games.

Among the choice of entertainment that people favour, is something called *Tambola*, also referred to as *Bingo*. In this, all the guests are handed small slips of paper with columns and rows made on it. Some numbers are printed on the squares, in a random manner, while a few are left blank.

These pieces of paper are sold at a set price and if you are not carrying any cash in your purse, then you have to begin by begging or borrowing the money – not a good way to start an evening.

Sitting in the front of the hall is a caller who calls out the numbers in a clear loud voice. The numerals that are announced have to be crossed out on the individual ticket that each person is

holding. The prizes are stated at the very beginning, and the winning rounds are for the fastest five, four corners, top line, bottom line and full house.

The numbers incidentally, are recited in a particular *bingolingo.* For me, if I ever get bullied into playing it, this is the only fun part of the game.

For instance, *two fat ladies is 88; in a fix is number 6; you are mine is number 9*; a *black raven is 27* and *wipe the slate is 78.*

If you are fortunate enough to have scratched all the lucky numbers on your ticket, then you shout out joyfully, and rush towards the caller, to claim your award.

Whenever I have played *Bingo*, however, I always lose. I don't know the reason but in any game where your blessed stars have to be good to you, mine simply get cross at me. So recently when I was unwillingly dragged into participating in one more game at a friend's place, I volunteered to become a caller.

"Son of a gun, number one," I announced, setting the ball rolling.

I had no idea about the rules so I invented them as I went along. Cooking up an impromptu rhyme to match the numbers was turning out to be more enjoyable than I thought.

But there was an irritating man in the first row. He squealed every time he got a correct response. As luck would have it, he won the first three prizes in quick succession and was gunning for a full house now.

"Rise and shine, 29," I sang out.

"Yes, Bingo!" the same man yelled, running towards me.

There was a disappointing silence in the room. I put my head down and cross checked. The error was in the last line and I disqualified him immediately.

"Many a slip between cups and lips is number six," I improvised warningly, enjoying the sound of my own voice.

Symptoms of Hypochondria

I have always been wary of dictionary meanings.
The precise description of objects and things leave me suspicious. I mean we all know that spade is a spade, and call it as such.

But here is what the glossary comes up with. 'A spade is a digging implement, a tool with a sharp edge, typically rectangular with a flat metallic blade or handle, adapted to push into the ground with the foot, used for digging earth or sand'. You get the idea?

The case with the word hypochondriac is similar. If one is to believe what the classic definition says, then it is described as 'a person with a chronic and abnormally excessive preoccupation with one's health, with the conviction that one is, or is likely to become ill, involving symptoms that are neither present nor persistent, despite medical assurance to the contrary'.

Now, this is just the kind of clarification that gets me instantly worried. Not to the point of calling the doctor, but it sends me scurrying into an Internet search immediately.

So, before self-diagnosing myself with a brand new disease, I wanted to make sure that it was indeed hypochondria that I was suffering from.

My family thought so, and some of my symptoms actually matched with the details of the disorder, but I believed that there was a possibility of error.

What if I was busy shrugging off the so-called ailments as a figment of my overactive imagination, and there was really a serious threat to my health? Then what? Who would be blamed for this oversight? Was it not better to err on the side of caution?

With this niggling thought in mind I made appointments with numerous specialists but more often than not, was shooed away after the initial investigation.

But as medical technology advanced, I found brand new genres to pick from. An Ophthalmologist, for instance, would not look at my throat. For that I would have to either go to an ENT expert or and Endocrinologist. Similarly, a Gastroenterologist was different from a Rheumatologist or a Cardiologist.

After being told that there was nothing wrong with me and I was wasting his time, by the last doctor I visited, I tried to overlook a blister that had formed on my finger.

But when the pain became unbearable my husband got concerned, and took me to a dermatologist. As soon as the physician walked in, I was taken aback. Tall and suave, he had the good looks of a film star.

"You can't be the doctor," I exclaimed.

"You can not be the patient," he mimicked.

"She has been ignoring this sore for sometime now," my husband interrupted, drawing out my hand for inspection.

The specialist got down to examining it, and then wrote out a prescription in detail.

"None of the domestic chores for you lady, no washing dishes, cooking, laundry, cleaning or mopping. Not even flower arrangement. This is an allergic reaction," he concluded.

"But she does not do any of those things," spouse said.

"Your wife is a glass house plant. You will not make her work," the doctor instructed sternly.

"So, what should be done?" my husband asked.

"Simply admire her," he ordered.

Whatever happens, I'm not giving up hypochondria in a hurry.

Bit of a Bargain

Women like to haggle.

It cuts across all ethnic and religious divides and binds us in some sort of universal sisterhood. I think it is inherent in our nature, and there is not much we can do about it.

If a certain price is offered for a product, we immediately try to bring it down. It is as if there is a higher authority that prompts us to behave in this manner.

It should come as no surprise therefore, that we drift towards open markets or souks that are manned by hawkers. Part of the attraction is the human interaction of course, but the added benefit is to get a best bargain out of the sale.

Bargaining is a talent. Or rather, it is a fine art, which is learnt on the job, so to speak. There are no guidebooks to help one master this accomplishment. At best, it is a trial and error process that requires patience, conversational proficiency and an ability to know how to walk away, or when to return.

As a youngster, whenever I trailed my mother or aunts during grocery shopping trips, I found myself in the role of a referee. To me it was like a game. The rules would be the same, only the players would be different.

They would start off by picking up anything, say a fruit or vegetable, or even a few grains of rice, and inquire about the cost. I would point at a hand written price list pasted on the wall, but was made to shut up with a stern look, or a severe smack on my knuckles.

Then the haggling took off in real earnest. The rate offered by the seller, would be sharply cut down by the buyer. The latter, quoting a new amount, would be met with exclamations of horror by the former.

I would do the calculations in my head furiously, and keep sympathising with whoever was getting a raw end of the deal. In most cases it was the hawker, and I would find myself on the wrong side of the fence.

My aunts would shoot killer looks at me and my poor knuckles would be quite sore by the end of the expedition.

After coming back home, I was given severe lectures on wasting my sympathy on crooks. I was also made to understand how I did not have the sense to pick a good bargain. At such moments I made a solemn promise to myself that I would never haggle over prices, when I grew up.

I kept my word all these years. And then I came to live in Amman.

Last week, in the midst of a crowded vegetable market I was busy buying spinach. The portly vendor prepared himself for the haggling to begin.

I agreed on the asking price, and saw his face fall.

He tried to hand me a bunch of greens.

"No, no, it's okay," I said, refusing the freebie.

"*Nana*? Here you go," he said, calling mint by its Arabic name.

"How much?" I asked

"For you, no extra charge beautiful lady. Just smile for me," he twinkled.

Basking in the unexpected compliment I was on cloud nine.

How to become a full-fledged haggler now?

American Tourist

Like most non-Americans my first impression of the United States was through books and movies and television shows.

The one I was partial to, called *The West Wing*, was based on the workings of the White House.

Whenever Hollywood presented a slice of American life, we as viewers, tried to identify with it. But in tragedy, comedy, suspense or romance, what clearly stood out in all the various films, was one common thing. And that was the eating habits of its citizens.

Or, to be more specific, the manner in which they ate.

From all the information that I had gathered, I figured that nobody in the US ever consumed his or her meals sitting around a dining table. The preferred places were: the sofa in front of a television screen, the kitchen counter facing a refrigerator, or the universal favourite of all: while walking.

The term used for *take-away* food, at any restaurant in America is, *on the go*. And so quite literally, a majority of meals were eaten while the individual was, on the go.

Coffee, milkshake, iced tea and juices, in fact all the possible drinks that can be poured into a large tumbler with a lid on top, were consumed, in a mobile state.

It did not matter what the scenario was. You could be visiting someone, entering a flight, exiting a hospital, rushing between meetings, or mowing a lawn. The most common sight in any American city was of people sipping out of a disposable cup.

Before my visit to the USA I religiously applied myself to two things.

First was, of course, the American drawl where one deliberately rolled a few consonants and smoothened out some vowels. For instance, running became *runnin* and understood became *unnerstood* and a sentence such as: 'you have not seen anything yet' got switched to, *'you ain't seen nothin' yet'*.

Secondly, I attempted to become one with the crowd by carrying a mug with me, at all times. So I drove to all the places in Amman like *Starbucks, McDonalds* and *KFC*. I ordered drinks for myself, both hot and cold, which were served to me in Styrofoam cups.

I learned to balance these in one hand while I steered the wheel of my car with the other one. Escaping the eagle eyed gaze of the traffic cops, I even managed to take small sips out of them.

The training went well and I was all set to blend in with the Americans as soon as I landed on foreign soil.

On the flight to Washington the crew was extremely friendly. The head stewardess was a New Yorker and kept smiling at me. I thought it was time to put my earlier drill into some use.

"Can I have a glass of water please?" I said in my most courteous voice.

"Sorry?" she asked politely.

"May I have a glass of water?" I repeated my request.

"Come again?" she countered, looking confused.

"My mom would like some *waderr*," my daughter drawled.

"Why didn't you say so *darlin*? *Comin'* right up," she exclaimed happily.

My dream of becoming an ideal American tourist died an instant death.

Pet Trainers

Today, all I did was make lists.

Before going on a holiday, this was the single most important thing to do, and it had to be done in a systematic manner.

I needed to buy gifts for family and friends that I would be visiting. But it was such a sham, this whole charade. I have yet to find anybody who is happy with his or her presents. They all pretend to be thrilled, but we know that it a useless formality, which should be done away with, immediately.

The minute I jotted something in a yellow post-it note, it disappeared into the dog's mouth, and was rolled into a spit bomb.

I reminded myself to speak to the dog trainer. He was training the dog and charging me a neat packet for it. But which command was I supposed to use to retract bits of paper? *Spit*? *Spit-Down*? *Spit-Down-Stay*? What was it exactly?

'*Spit*' sounded so much like '*sit*' that every time I tried it, coupled with the stern expression I was taught to use, the dog sat down and grinned at me. With ears folded back, his expression begged for a juicy treat. It was not nice to confuse a dog like this.

But it was more a training for the pet owners, than the actual pets. This I had realised in the last several sessions with Ron, our South African dog trainer.

He kept issuing orders at me, while saying nothing to the dog.

I must look for signs, he said. If the dog was not listening to me, I should change the tone of my voice. If he jumped around

endlessly, it meant that he was lonely. In that case, I should shower my undivided attention on him. If he chewed my shoes, I must simply buy new ones for myself.

After going through his usual drone of directives for me, I cornered Ron with my problem. He had just arrived to administer training to our dog.

"You mean he chewed up the notepad completely? It contained your shopping list? What a shame! You poor thing," Ron said, shaking his head.

I thought he was sympathizing with me, till I noticed he was communicating with the dog.

"You want to make him spit out what he has chewed? That is a very difficult job. But you are such an intelligent dog, aren't you, sweetie? Can teach you to do anything, your breed is so sharp, isn't it lovely? We will learn something new today, won't we gorgeous?" Ron kept crooning to the dog.

Let's see then, "*Spit!*" he commanded.

The dog sat down happily.

"*Sit?* No, no," Ron pulled him up roughly with the leash.

"Listen carefully, *Spit!*" Ron made a motion with his mouth.

The dog sat down again.

"So tough, this language is. If I could talk to him in Afrikaans, it would be so much easier," Ron glared at me, as if it was entirely my fault.

"Let us try again, *Spit!*" he said forcefully, trying to keep the dog's jaw open with his hand.

The canine closed his mouth over Ron's fingers sharply.

"Aw, *Shit!*" he howled in pain, swearing profanities.

The dog sat down obediently, with a joyful grin.

Let me just say that I never managed to retrieve my list.

Pain in the Neck

One has to suffer from pain in the neck, to understand a pain in the neck.

I mean there is no simpler way of describing it, other than inflicting it severely upon whoever asks you the dumb question.

With many of us getting inclined towards alternative treatments for various sicknesses, the pharmaceutical companies are having a field day.

In a chemist shop, one now has a choice between Chinese *'capsicum bandages'* for curing arthritis, or acupressure slippers for healing rheumatism. The latest to arrive in the sure cure arena is the fully contoured, and orthopedically approved, *'medi-pillow'*.

After years of nursing a 'stiff neck,' I was the first to spot the generous advertisement in the local paper. This new device made claims of having treated the unhappiest of cases, and I was eager to have a go at it.

When I called the listed number, I was informed that the chemist shop selling the wonder pillow was located in downtown Amman. With grim determination I set off towards my destination, and a couple of hours later, I was lost in the maze of lanes and by-lanes.

Impatiently, I crawled in and out of the confusing muddle, and finally spotted the signboard on the opposite side of *'Joy Tailors'*.

Ahmed, the pharmacist, was having his evening tea and was

not in a mood to talk. He took his time sipping the brew, and studied me without speaking. Then he casually took a walk around.

Finally, he looked up, and immediately recognised the paper cutting I passed him.

"You want to see the contour pillow?" he asked suspiciously.

"The medical pillow," said my spouse.

"Same thing," he beamed.

"You, a pain in the neck?" he inquired, looking straight at me.

"She gets a pain in the neck," my husband corrected.

"Same thing," he beamed again.

Next he disappeared behind a door marked '*no admission*'. A few minutes later he emerged carrying a rectangular packet with colourful graphic designs on it.

"Made in England, see?" Ahmed showed us the label.

"Englishmen suffer from arthritis, rheumatism, back pain and stiff neck all the time. This takes care of everything and the aches and pains simply disappear. Believe me, it should actually be called a magic pillow. Very good for migraine also," Ahmed recited.

"You, a pain in the head?" he asked my spouse this time.

"She's the one who gets all these weird attacks. I don't know what a headache feels like!" my husband boasted.

Ahmed then transferred all his attention onto me. He pointed out the neck curve, and the contoured depression on the side of the pillow. These supposedly helped to support the spine while lying on the back.

"Just use it for four continuous days without fail and you'll notice the difference on the fifth day itself," Ahmed instructed,

"See for yourself how miraculous it is, and you will come back to thank me," he kept talking, while I did the payment.

"And you," he said, shaking my spouse by the hand. "You just give me a call if she is still a pain in the neck."

The Talking Gene

'A brilliant conversationalist is one who is adept in the art of using meaningless words to say a lot about nothing.'

I read this out aloud from a book gifted to me by Sharon, a friend of mine. A little unkindly, "she must have taken this observation a bit too much to heart," said the voice in my head.

I remember the talk I had with her just before she handed me the book.

"Go through it. It's very entertaining, and will help you with all the blah, blah, blah," she told me enthusiastically.

Sharon was one of those people who crammed too much into too little. An ordinary day was not enough for her to accomplish all that she set out to do from the moment she woke up.

A full-fledged career woman on the brink of a fabulous promotion, mother of a demanding two year old, and a hectic socialite, Sharon was all that, and more. She tried to hold on to her sanity, but cracks were beginning to appear. This was most noticeable when she got talking, especially in her manner of speaking.

Her main area of concern was her toddler. An adorable moppet-with dark curls tumbling over his head-her son was a reluctant speaker.

"This child will just not talk," she complained in exasperation.

"I took him to the best speech therapist in Jordan, and all he could tell me was blah, blah, blah," she moaned.

"What did he say?" I asked her.

Sharon was confused.

"The specialist," I prompted.

"I just told you, he said we should learn to relax and not push the kid into any kind of stress and blah, blah, blah," Sharon explained in her inimitable manner.

A fast talker, her words would constantly come out in a rush because of a stuttering disorder she overcame in her adolescence. She felt that if she did not speak quickly, she might start stammering, once more.

But the 'blah, blah, blah' syndrome was newly acquired, and most of the time I could not make head or tail of what she said.

Overworked and easily irritable, Sharon did not like to be called an eccentric.

"What is wrong with everyone?" she grumbled the other day. "I have to keep repeating, and nobody seems to get me right. I told my housemaid, for the third time, what to buy from the supermarket, and she is still standing here right in front of me. Maybe she does not understand English," she fumed.

"What did you ask for?" I asked.

"To get the usual, blah, blah, blah," Sharon clarified.

But somehow, she shared a perfect rapport with her husband. He was the only one who could understand her bizarre speaking pattern, and found nothing awkward in it.

One day, a wonderful thing happened. Their two year old finally found his voice and Sharon was ecstatic. She immediately requested me to speak to the little one on the phone.

"He will sing a nursery rhyme for you, do not do any blah, blah, blah, just listen to him," she ordered.

"Blah, Blah, Black Sheep," a childish treble started reciting.

Like mother like son?

My Experiments with Truth

I have been trying an experiment since the crack of dawn today, and I am determined to make a success of it.

Well, at least, for as long as it lasts. I am going to speak the truth and nothing but the truth!

There, I've said it aloud. No more white lies for me, no more hiding the facts, and no more calling a day anything but diurnal.

My morning passed without much discomfort, though I belatedly noticed my housemaid going about her job without much enthusiasm. I told her that my tea was lukewarm, which it was. I also pointed out that she should cut the fruits properly because all the pieces in my breakfast plate were not symmetrical.

Pleased with my progress, I informed the gardener that he was not mowing the lawn regularly. Brushing his protests aside, I told him to be more careful in the future, and went on to lecture him on the benefits of speaking the truth, under all circumstances.

Later, I went to my gym class and met up with my old buddies. One of them asked me if I thought her South Beach Diet was showing results. I said I didn't think so, because her belly was still too large, and though her face had shrunk, premature wrinkles had marred it.

I saw her blink twice to register my brutal answer, but it made no impact on me because I was on this mission, you see?

I told her that all the weight-loss fads were nonsensical, and that she always looked fatter right after she went on a diet. And then, before I could tell her about further health risks, she abruptly turned and left me standing there, in mid sentence.

Shrugging off the uneasy feeling at having upset a friend, I persisted. "Truth Hurts," I reasoned. "You have to be cruel to be kind," I said to myself.

Coming home I heard the phone ringing, and just as I was racing towards it, I saw my domestic help pick it up.

"Ma'am is in the bathroom," she mumbled at the handset, in the time honoured tradition of white lies that I had taught her.

"No, no, I am right here," I said, picking up the extension.

"It's just what she is supposed to tell people I don't want to speak to," I explained earnestly, to my caller.

Suddenly the telephone receiver went dead, and no amount of 'hello, hello' could retrieve the connection for me.

By now I was beginning to get worried.

All was not going well in my truth-experimenting world. Though nobody said anything outright, I did not like the reactions my true-speak was generating. Nevertheless, I blundered on.

My husband came home with a fresh haircut that looked awful. I told him so. My daughter asked me if her scarlet nail polish colour looked nice. I said it was garish and completely over the top.

I saw sullen faces, flashing eyes, surly manner and hasty disappearances. In a nutshell, nobody liked hearing the truth because these days no one says what he or she wishes to say. Everyone just tells you what you want to hear.

Being tactful was accepted, but being truthful was not.

I learnt an important lesson, and trying to hold on to my remaining friends, I started making hasty amends.

Right away!

Portrait of a Gentleman

Two things happened this week.

By themselves they would not have surprised me. But occurring one after another, in quick succession, they got me thinking.

First, when I was backing my car from a parking lot, a man helped me to manoeuver it.

He was a stranger, who was about to cross the road. But when he saw me struggling with the vehicle, he stopped to give helpful suggestions. As soon as I got out of the tight spot, he went away, acknowledging my thanks with a slight nod.

Later in the day I was standing in a queue at a grocery store. The person behind me was dressed in a business suit, and was talking loudly on his cellphone. Suddenly, he pushed his supermarket trolley over my foot.

I yelped in pain and hopped around, but he didn't even notice it. Simply ignoring the scene he had caused, he kept speaking into the handset.

These twin incidents, where two people of the same gender behaved in such a contrasting manner, made me curious about the qualities that defined a gentleman. Was chivalry completely dead? Were polite men extinct?

I decided to quiz some women to find out what was more important, courtesy or honesty? Did impeccable manners, and consideration for others, total up to good behavior? Armed with these queries, I confronted the other sisters of my tribe.

"Who says the age of chivalry is dead? These days if a girl drops her books, a boy kicks them back to her," laughed my friend, when I put her through the interrogation.

"A gentleman should be gracious, intelligent, talented, confident, well dressed, and culturally aware," my gym instructor told me.

"Also, respectful towards everyone, especially women," added an elegant lady, who overheard our conversation.

"In an ideal world, men ought to be chivalrous," insisted my old school teacher.

"Despite women's lib, men should never forget the basic rules of etiquette. They must open doors to cars, restaurants, offices or homes. Help a lady with her coat. Give up their seat for mothers with children or the elderly. Get a woman seated, before sitting down in a restaurant," she continued, warming up to the theme.

"Be punctual, shake hands firmly, never flaunt your riches," a young waitress supplied.

"Use polite terms like *excuse me*, *thank you*, *please* and *I beg your pardon*. Never remove their coat or necktie in public. During dinner, address the people sitting at both your left, and right," interjected a tall blonde woman.

"Not interrupt when someone else is speaking, pay the bill as discretely as possible," emphasised the Blondie.

Once the floodgates were opened, the answers came flying at breakneck speed. My survey seemed to have stirred up a hornet's nest.

After the dust had settled over the storm that I had unwittingly unleashed, I asked them to name a potential winner for the most gentlemanly gentleman's title.

I am happy to report that Barack Obama and James Bond shared a winning tie.

So, we still do have, a few good men.

Out of the Frying Pan

People who enjoy cooking insist it de-stresses them.
I hate cooking because it stresses me out. This is not to say that I don't cook. It's just that I don't relish it.

For enjoyment purposes, I earmark other more pleasurable activities like reading, walking, shopping or arguing. But to my utter discomfort, I get emotionally blackmailed into stirring the wok, every few days.

That is because my family thinks, much to my utter astonishment that I cook wonderfully.

Going along with this fallacy, I decided to surprise my husband on his birthday with his favourite dish. For this particular culinary delicacy, I had to prepare, three days in advance. A South Indian cuisine called *dosa* is something that is shaped like a pancake, and is staple food there.

Now to enjoy Indian food, one has to know a little bit about India, which is divided into two broad regions. The people living in these areas are completely different in the language they speak, the foods they eat, the clothes they wear, and so on.

The North Indians and the South Indians enjoy a relationship of mutual snobbery. The ones in the North think that they are more lively, fun loving, and fashion conscious. The Southerners believe they are better educated, more cultured, and disciplined. According to them, the North Indians are loud, kitschy show offs, while the former feel that the latter are dull, nerdish and unexciting.

In such a scenario, everybody co-exists by simply minding their own business. Which works fine, but sometimes, in a rare show of camaraderie, we borrow a page from one another's recipe books. That is when the problems arise, because the dishes that are made routinely in one kitchen can be a real challenge in the other.

In my misplaced enthusiasm, I decided to make a *dosa*. It was an uphill task all the way. One wrong manoeuver, and the entire dish could end up in disaster.

So, I had to first soak the rice and lentil combination in the exact mathematical proportion of three is to one. The next morning, I had to grind it into a fine paste, mix it all together and leave it to ferment. For the entire day, that is.

Come dinner time, my two helpers, the cook and the housemaid, flanked me on both sides. They watched unblinkingly as I warmed a flat girdle on the fire.

The last time, when the *dosa* had stuck to it like glue, the cook had declared the pan to be faulty. I had insisted the mixture he put together, was incorrect.

Therefore, here I was, giving a demonstration, with the ingredients that I had prepared myself. I was nervous as hell. It was a moment of reckoning that would make or mar my reputation.

I spooned the gooey paste and spread it, fanning it outwards in a clockwise manner. My two helpers were motionless in rapt attention. I closed my eyes and murmured a silent prayer.

The mix would either stick stubbornly, or peel off nicely.

Taking a deep breath to steady myself, I peeped though half opened lids. Right there, in front of me, was a perfect *dosa*. I was as flabbergasted as my cook. And the maid could not stop smiling.

But the stress was more than I could handle. To make up for it, I went shopping the next day.

Lost and Found

The thing is, I am always losing stuff.

Not misplacing it, mind you. That I do too, like putting the house keys in one bag and looking for it in a host of other ones till I wilt in exhaustion. Or, the more recently acquired habit of forgetting where I placed my reading glasses, and going round the bend, searching for it.

I am used to this condition, but it's different when something is irretrievably gone and lost forever.

The first time it happened in a taxicab.

I opened my purse to take out my wallet, but after paying the fare, instead of putting it back I left it on the seat itself. Or so it seemed, when I tried to recall the sequence of events later on.

But here is the strange thing. Before I could even begin the process of erasing my identity by canceling my credit and debit cards, it was retrieved.

The cabbie appeared at the reception desk of the hotel I was staying in, and returned my wallet. I tried to give him money for his efforts, but he mumbled something incoherent, and vanished.

I realised later that he had tipped himself rather generously on my behalf, but other than the loss of some currency, everything else was intact. In fact, even my twenty-four hour *hop-on hop-off* bus ticket was left untouched.

Soon, I dropped my wallet again. In a taxi, that's right. But this instance, it took several days to find its way to the original

owner. Buoyed by the success of the first retrieval that worked in my favour, I was sure this one would come back to me too.

So, I gave myself one week to do nothing, other than bite my nails to the quick. On the seventh day, I found a square shaped packet in my letter box. Nothing was missing, not even the cash.

Was it divine intervention, or were people just becoming more honest in their dealings with me? I don't know.

Subsequently, I lost the following articles: a cell-phone, a gold bracelet, eighty pounds, an ivory coloured stole, oversized sunglasses, and a ruby red lipstick. Eventually, virtual strangers returned all of these items to me. Within a span of few days, that is.

The goodness of the universe knows no bounds, and I am sure it is just a numbers game. My good fortune might soon run out, but I have not had much to complain about, till now.

The other day I was buying some fresh fruit juice, in a crowded food court. A talkative man behind the counter tried to strike a conversation with me, but I was distracted, and kept answering in monosyllables.

He handed me the tumbler, and just as I turned to go, he called out to me in a loud voice.

"Hey lady, you forgot this," he said, reaching his arm out, as if returning something.

"My wallet? Again?" I exclaimed in disbelief.

"No, no! You had lost your smile, here it is," he said, grinning wickedly, and tapped my palm with his fingertips.

Finding it instantly, I beamed back in response.

Tips and Toes

Where women and beauty is concerned, one thing is for sure, no woman is happy with the way she looks.

Take it from me. I know this.

It is not that we are generally unhappy with our entire appearance. But given a choice, we would like a few adjustments: thicker hair, higher cheekbones, smoother skin, larger eyes, and so on.

It is on this, our very primal, and basic insecurity that the whole beauty business thrives. And the professional careers of plastic surgeons worldwide also hinge on the same premise. Yes, it is a conspiracy against the fairer sex, a psychological tool of sorts.

It is quite sad really, because we know that we are getting conned and the highly overpriced beauty products might not deliver on half the promises their marketing slogans announce. Yet we buy them.

It might be false vanity, but I call it true optimism. We never give up hope, you see. And sometimes it works wonders. No, not the fancy creams in their fancier jars, but the eternal hope in our optimistic hearts.

Reem works in *Polish*. It is a place where women go to get their hands and feet polished. The process starts with the nails being soaked and scrubbed, followed by clipping of the cuticles, buffering the edges, and finally a coat of varnish applied to the finished product. It is not as simple as it sounds. It requires hard work and dedication but Reem does the job with skillful ease.

Reem has perfect nails. She is the proud owner of a set of exceptionally polished and pampered '*tips and toes*'. In oval shape, they are painted in stunning shades of red, pink or orange when she is on a high. She switches the colours to muted baby pinks or buff browns when she is feeling low. It is a good barometer of her moods.

The latest gossip doing the rounds in the city reaches her first, before anyone even gets to know about it. It's incredible how Reem is clued onto all the scandalous rumours, sitting within the four walls of her beauty salon.

"It's first hand information," she hisses at me everytime, when I look shocked.

"Straight from the horse's mouth," she will insist if I still look unconvinced.

The various bottles of hand-lotions, nail-shampoos, and knuckle softeners that she markets have her personal signature on them. They cost a neat fortune but on each visit, I end up buying some. Initially, I was not interested in parting with colossal sums of money to cultivate a hand-feet makeover. I never really felt the need to.

I mean hands were for shaking, and a warm handshake demonstrates more about a person's personality than a prettily painted one.

Big mistake, I was told. Reem claimed that every woman needed perfect hand and feet maintenance. To look like a lady, that is. It was hard to argue with her and so I bought all her potions.

The one I liked best was the green 'revitalizing cream' that had crushed aspirins, ground mint and dried papaya powder in it.

"Guaranteed to beautify the ugliest of paws, just wait and see," Reem informed me as she applied the gooey stuff all over my hands.

What can I say? I'm still waiting. For miracles to happen!

Mothers and Daughters

I belong to a part of the world that longs for sons.

Deny it as much as we want, the statistics show that where offspring is concerned, Indians prefer to have boys.

It is a fact that is proven right time and again in the various demographical surveys. The craving for a male progeny stretches across the entire fabric of our society: from the snobbish upper class, to the educated middle class, percolating even to the economically deprived lower class.

There are varied reasons for this. Without going into too much detail, let me just say that even in this modern age, if a couple has two or more daughters, and no son, they are secretly pitied. I have met and interacted with scores of families who feel this way.

Unfortunately, and here is the heartbreaking part, many women, who are mothers-in-law, sisters-in-law and their ilk, encourage other females to engage in all sorts of malpractices, in order to get a boy child.

The reverse case, where families with many sons yearn for a daughter, also occurs, but such scenarios are extremely rare. Even then, it is only after a third son is born that a daughter is finally desired, if at all.

A college friend, who is a post-grad from a prestigious university, shakes his head in embarrassment while announcing the birth of his baby. She happens to be his first child, but she is a '*girl child*' you see, and hence the disappointment.

"I was at the hospital along with my father when my wife went into labour," he recalls.

"When I heard the infant cry it sounded like a boy and we congratulated each other," he explains.

"But then the nurse came out of the delivery room and said that I had a baby girl. I took a deep breath and collapsed on the nearest chair," he confides mournfully.

This scene recurs in most homes.

The arrival of a son is greeted with merriment while that of a daughter with restrained sorrow. The mother goes through the same birth pangs, but the gender of the delivered baby is the most important criteria in determining the levels of celebration.

I love daughters. They are prettier to look at and personify *John Keats'* line: '*a thing of beauty is a joy for ever*'.

Despite what the pattern of my home country dictates, I think couples that don't have daughters are a deprived lot. They miss out on a whole lot of caring, gentleness, tenderness, devotion, appreciation, kindness, warmth, concern and affection that flows naturally through them.

Our daughter has been a permanent source of happiness for me.

From the moment I held her in my arms as a warm bundle, she has continually delighted me, as a mother. When she was little, I longed for her to grow up fast, so that I could have conversations with her. But once she started talking non-stop, I have to keep urging her to be quiet.

Her biggest grudge with me over the years is that she is never mentioned in my stories.

"When will you write about me Mom?" is her constant complaint.

This September, impulsively I decided to lift my self-imposed restriction to grant her request.

From a mother to a daughter: happy birthday!

Holy Matrimony

Like all married women I have given serious and generous thought to how much I have contributed towards my matrimonial well being.

After all, a marriage is only as robust as its participants are.

Recently I completed twenty-five years of wedded bliss. On paper it appears an entire lifetime, but when I look back, it seems only yesterday that I entered into this holy alliance.

There are two kinds of people in this world: those who know where their wedding album is and those who do not. I do not.

Even if I did, I would have to try very hard to find some resemblance between the extra skinny newly weds of then, and the two of us now. But what strikes out very clearly in those pictures is that we were absolutely delighted at getting married.

What is the secret of a happy marriage? Do nuptials automatically lead to a state of happiness? Should one marry to be happy or should one be happy to be married?

There are no straightforward answers to these questions but various surveys prove that married men live longer than their unmarried counterparts. They also enjoy better physical and mental health because their wives nag them. Nagging wives is an added asset, because they badger their husbands to exercise, adopt a healthier lifestyle and take fewer risks.

But every time I read out these published statistics to my spouse, he shook his head with disbelief. He claimed that men or women, both married and single, were very capable of looking after themselves. Given a chance, they could switch roles of provider and nurturer with equal ease, he told me.

To check if there was any truth to it, I decided to do a trial. After two decades of routinely buying the groceries, I handed my husband the shopping list. On seeing it, he immediately got a flustered look on his face and started making excuses.

They were as varied as they were imaginative.

Did I not understand that he had important conferences to attend and influential people to meet? It's not that he had anything against going to a grocery store, *per se*, but could I not see that he was constrained by time?

My sad expression made him relent, somewhat. He promised that he would see what he could manage to buy, on the way back from work.

At seven pm sharp I got the first call.

"So, tell me the two most essential things on your list and I will get them," my spouse announced magnanimously.

"Bread and Milk," I said

Fifteen minutes later my phone rang again.

"You want white bread, brown bread, whole grain bread, Soya bread, milk bread or olive bread," asked my husband.

"Also, should it be jumbo size, mini size, sandwich size or toast size," he inquired.

As soon as I settled that there was another call.

"This loaf of bread, should it be sliced, un-sliced or a baguette?" he quizzed.

His next call was timed almost immediately.

"The milk that I have to buy, should it be full fat, half fat, skimmed or semi-skimmed? And, there is fresh milk, long life milk, powdered milk, condensed milk also on the shelf," he went on.

Marriages are made in heaven? Right?

Kitchen Times

The kitchen, which till quite recently was the most central part of any household, is fast losing its importance.

Women who were traditionally considered the ones looking after the hearth have become more caught up in their professional careers. So, eating out has replaced home cooked meals.

Most modern couples go for days without bothering to eat in.

There are a lot of reasons for this: a wider variety of food to choose from, no hassles of tackling the dirty dishes, and no buying the ingredients to make the tedious effort of cooking it.

Ordering a take-away is also an option. A phone call is all it takes, for the food of choice, to be delivered right at your doorstep. And you don't even have to dress for dinner.

If everything can be handed on a platter, why do people still build kitchens in their homes? Does it even make sense any more? A microwave and a fridge is all that one needs to heat the ordered food, and store the leftovers. So, will the architectural designs of future communities do away with this space altogether? Is that what we are headed towards?

In my house the kitchen occupies a very dominant place. It is also the busiest of rooms. Aromatic smells and interesting sounds originate from it all the time. From the cauldron and kettle, to the frying pan, all the utensils are used in regular rotation, to produce wholesome food for the family.

Unfortunately, I could never take to cooking like my mom or

grandmother. They tried, during various stages of my upbringing, to instill a fondness for stirring the pot, but failed. I was a miserable learner. I could, sort of, grasp the broader picture, but when they tried to pass on the secret family recipes, I would lose interest almost immediately.

But life is a great teacher, and shortly I learned how to wield the rolling pin, so to speak. What I did not imagine, even in my wildest dreams, is how much my cooking would be appreciated. Despite it being an activity that gave me panic attacks, I ended up becoming rather good at it.

Yet, as soon as I could afford a cook, I hired one and kept a safe distance between the kitchen and me. But yesterday, I had to re-enter this unknown territory. The chef was ill, and I had a family to feed.

So I designed a simple menu and went about preparing it. The pots and pans were banged extra hard to give vent to my irritation.

A drop of oil flew out of the wok to form a blister in my arm, which did not help matters. But as the dishes took form and shape I started to feel better.

At the dinner table there were gasps of delight.

"You made this?" my husband asked.

"Why?" I was ready to pick a fight.

"It is delicious Mom," my daughter reassured.

"Superb! What ingredients did you add?" spouse exclaimed.

"The usual," I mumbled.

"Is it possible to prevent the cook from recovering?" our little one wanted to know.

"When the chef resumes work, could you still pick out one day of the week to make dinner?" they requested.

My next plan of action is concocted out of sheer desperation. In the coming days, I intend to spoil the broth.

The Bore Connection

These days, it is not difficult to be a bore. In fact I would add that it is the easiest thing in the world, and requires no particular skill, other than being boring.

Who is a bore? In its simplest form, it's a term used for persons who inspires boredom. The word '*inspire*' could be misleading here, because that is a positive expression with undertones of motivation, encouragement and enthusiasm. But these merits, unfortunately, are completely lacking in a bore.

Boredom itself is a state that one gets into as a result of being weary and restless, through lack of interest. Yet, one thing is for sure, it is a great leveler, and has people from every community, irrespective of their age, gender or nationality, succumbing to it. Such is the extensive spread of the malaise that there is hardly anyone who is not touched by it. At some point or the other in their lives, that is.

What could possibly be the reason behind this? Does it have anything to do with a lack of concentration? Or do we universally suffer from an absence of focus? Is our attention span getting shorter? What exactly is attention span?

The phrase, in my opinion, is used to describe the time-period during which one can be attentive towards anything or anyone, without being distracted.

With the arrival of smart-phones, social network sites, and Internet, the means of our disturbance has increased and our attention span, decreased. Research reveals that it has now reduced to an all time low figure of seven seconds. Let me repeat that: seven, lonesome, seconds!

It is in those seven abysmal seconds of being able to hold anybody's attention that one has to learn to interact, in a fast and effective manner. The rest is all a gigantic waste. Unnecessary repetition of a point gets one relegated into being a bore anyway.

Incidentally, I was never allowed to grow up to become a bore. When I was very young, even its utterance was banned in my house. My mother detested the term strongly, and clubbed it together with the other unspeakable four letter words.

A whispered, under the breath exclamation, could also get us grounded for a lengthy period of time. Her ears sadly, were extremely sharp and very often I had to swallow the expression even before it left my mouth. To be bored or boring was a fate worse than death. Well, almost.

And so, to bluff her, my siblings and I invented a decoy word. We would say we were *tired* whenever we were *bored*. Any *boring* person became a *tiring* one.

The result was that for an entire decade, all our mother could hear from us was our description of tiredness. To make up for this imaginary shortcoming, she force-fed us gazillions of fish liver oil, by the spoonsful. But in certain situations, we continued to be, tired.

Years later we tried the trick word, one more time.

When I called my brother the other day, he was in an important business meeting. Our time zones did not match so he agreed to quickly speak to me from his conference room itself.

"How is it going?" I greeted.

"Very tiring," he said.

"You are ill?" I was concerned.

"No, just tired, you know, the other one," he giggled.

"Ah! Tire them back," I laughed, encrypting it in a flash.

"What are you guys laughing about?" asked my husband, listening in on the speakerphone.

"Nothing!" we chorused.

The bore connection persists!

How to Win Friends

What do I do when someone sends me a friend request? On Facebook, that is.

Well, I usually peer at the name and the accompanying display picture. If the list of *mutual friends* that is helpfully provided is more than twenty, I accept it. A click of the mouse is all it takes and it's done. One more friend is added.

But it was not always so. There was a time we had to pore over books like *How to win friends and influence people* by *Dale Carnegie*. It had gems like 'fundamental techniques in handling individuals' and 'six ways to make people like you'.

Putting his suggestions into practice was a slow and torturous process.

But what it taught us was that broadly speaking, friends are of two types, the selfless givers, versus the selfish takers. I desperately wanted to be of the former variety, but honesty compels me to admit that I fall in the latter category. How do I know this?

Here is a list of my sins: I forget names within the first five minutes of meeting new people; I nod off if a person gets started on a boring monologue; I don't remember to tip taxi drivers unless they glower at me threateningly, and if there is a last piece of chocolate left in the wrapper, I am the first one to eat it.

In fact, once I was so annoyed at my house guest who was generously helping herself to my overpriced lotion with a sun protection factor of 50, that I went to the nearest store and bought

her a cheap sun-hat. She doubled up with appreciation and kept thanking me profusely. I accepted the gratitude without any qualms.

Despite my absent-minded indifference, I am blessed with a supportive group of friends. They are loyal and help me to hold my head high, also making sure that my feet are firmly planted on the ground. So caring and thoughtful are they that, at times, I feel I don't deserve them. But fond memories of a common childhood ensure that we stay bonded.

Recently, one of them lectured me, on giving back to the community. You know, like feed the hungry, organize a charity or do something for the underprivileged people.

Eventually, from a list of ideas that veered from mundane to the ridiculous I was persuaded into taking some classes in a school. It was to be a sort of workshop for the students and I was to conduct it for free.

The day dawned nice and bright when I left home. But once I approached the campus, my gait slowed down. It had been quite a while since I had last been anywhere near an institution of learning.

Soon I was in a classroom but I was facing the other way this time. My flashcards were in front of me and I was looking forward to interacting with young minds.

The childish chatter ceased as I walked in, and all of them stood up to greet me. Before I could start the talk, a hand went up.

"Ma'am, are you on Facebook?" asked a well-modulated voice that belonged to a fresh-faced teenager.

"Yes, of course," I smiled.

"Can I send you a friend request?" he entreated.

Within minutes more hands were up. All of them had the same query.

I rejected my well-prepared lecture and impulsively veered the discussion into new mass media, and the power of Internet communication.

Dale Carnegie would be proud of me. By the end of the day, I had made fifty new friends.

War of the Roses

One might almost call it a war of the roses.

It all started quite innocently. One fine day, I decided to plant a rose garden. Actually it began a bit before that, the battle, that is.

I noticed a little expanse of land on one side of my house. It had been tended beautifully and verdant grass lined it like a thick and luxuriant carpet. But then I spotted a patchy corner that was ridden with weeds, and crying for attention.

I decided to send for Hanif from the local gardening store. He was an ace gardener and I needed his expert opinion on what to do with my wasteland.

Hanif cancelled two appointments and then suddenly arrived at my doorstep in the middle of a busy weekday.

Before he could start the inspection, I tried coaxing him to suggest to my husband to have only rose-cuttings planted. I could have done it myself, but they came at a phenomenally expensive price. Added to the cost of the fertiliser and topsoil, I would end up spending a fortune. This definitely needed the intervention of Hanif, and his persuasion skills, at getting my spouse to approve the venture.

But first, I had to convince Hanif that a rose garden is what the house needed, preferably the variety of roses that came from Holland.

Now, Hanif did not like being told what to do, least of all by a woman. I knew that from our earlier interaction. For him, the man was the supreme head of a household and his decision was paramount. So, all the while I took him around the garden path, he kept looking for something, or rather someone.

"Where is *Sayyidi?*" he asked me suddenly, using the Arabic expression for *Sir*.

I had lived in this part of the world long enough to realise he was referring to my husband.

"I want to talk to *Sayyidi*. He told me to get some colourful petunias and marigolds for the flower bed," he announced.

"That's what I'm telling you. Petunias and marigold don't look half as good as roses. You tell him to have a rose bush done instead," I argued.

"But Madam, roses will take more than a month to bloom, and they wither away in the next," he said, talking slowly, as if explaining to a child. "You better wait for *Sayyidi*. He said get petunias and marigolds and I think he made the right choice."

I was seething with annoyance but Hanif took no notice of me.

He went for a leisurely stroll in the various patches of green around my house and did some mental calculations.

"When is *Sayyidi* getting here," he asked me impatiently.

"I need his permission to fix the backyard kitchen garden also. It is in a royal mess," he scowled.

"Who said anything about the kitchen garden?" I was very irritated by now.

"You go ahead and plant the rose garden first. I'm giving you the total responsibility," I declared.

"But *Sayyidi* is the head of the house-hold. He will decide, and you must listen to him," Hanif lectured me, glaring in disapproval.

"Really? Your *Sayyidi* might be the head, but I'm the neck that shakes the head, so you better get going. Now, now!" I finalised the deal with a click of my fingers.

Battle and war, both won!

Birthday Blues

The good thing about being born in the first month of the Gregorian calendar is that one's birth gets celebrated along with the New Year revelry.

There is enough spill-over from the festivities to, sort of, tide you through.

I mean the merrymaking season does not fully subside until then. So, the twinkling lights, fancy tableware, half opened drinks and leftover snacks, can all be gathered together and put to good use.

It is a neat little trick, and even the disposable crockery and cutlery comes in handy. The dance floor is ready for further utilization and the choice of music that was previously uploaded can be re-used.

When I was little, my mother was an expert at it. In fact I would daresay this was her particular area of super specialisation.

Not only did she consider my birthday a continuation of the New Year Eve's party, but she clubbed my older sibling's date of birth celebrations along with all of this too. It was no fault of ours, other than both of us sharing the same month of arrival into this world.

Nobody could hold us responsible for this, because we hardly had any say in that matter.

Our mum used to pick a weekend, roughly between the actual birthdays of the two of us, to a have joint party. She was under the

mistaken impression that by inviting all his friends along with mine, we would have a gala time.

This displeased both of us immensely, because by sharing the limelight, it reduced the importance of the event. My brother insisted it was his birthright to open all my presents. And I was adamant about cutting his birthday cake along with mine, one knife balanced precariously in each hand.

If, for some reason, I could not manage that, then I would immediately blow out the candles on his cake, before I did mine. The end result, I am sad to report, was always unhappy.

We were packed off to our rooms, and our hapless father would be left wondering what went wrong.

Since there were no psychoanalytical counsellors available during that period, it took my parents quite a few years to figure out how to keep the family harmony, and have separate parties for us. Even though it meant twice the effort.

Lately, by some quirk of fate, I stumbled upon my old school group on a social media site. This lively cast of men and women keep up a sense of constant bonhomie round the clock by posting pictures, anecdotes, sports updates and melodious songs on the forum.

Crisscrossing the length and breadth of the globe, their musings about the bygone days bring my childhood memories alive. I've not had one dull moment since I reconnected with them.

To help chase my birthday blues, last year they organised a school reunion, which coincided with my date of birth.

My past experiences being what they were, I was quite used to the event becoming an amalgam of other joint festivities.

But when it came to blowing the candles out, nothing had changed. It still remained very much, my prerogative.

So, what was my birthday wish? To have my cake, and eat it too!

Empty Threats

Certain places are awe-inspiring.

Walking through the enclosure of a historical building, for instance, or studying the minute and intricate carvings on an old relic. The utter majesty it possesses, humbles you instantly.

Incidentally, being awed is quite different from getting intimidated. The former term, to the best of my knowledge, is a positive fear. If fright can be so labelled, that is.

It involves being impressed or overwhelmed. But the latter phrase has negative connotations written all over it. It means being nervous, anxious and tense, all at the same time.

During my childhood, there were several things that could cause me to break out in cold sweat. In school, the mere mention of being sent to the headmistress's office would bring an anxiety attack. The angelic nuns could, with a simple curl of the upper lip, instil dread upon us hapless students. Being made to witness that was a fate worse than death.

The guilt trip that they made you incur, was another story altogether. How our shortcomings became a cause for their anguish is something I have yet to figure out.

Other stuff that scared me were, elaborate five star hotel lobbies, check-in counters of large airports, and sign boards announcing '*police station*'.

Hospital wards, men and women in military uniform and darkened cinema theatres, where my earliest memory is of sitting with my back towards the big screen, frightened me too. And of course, trips to the barber.

In those days the barbers had sharp scissors which they liked to click continuously, even between trims. My biggest dread was that they would cut off my ear if I did not sit absolutely still on the high chair. This empty threat would keep me on my best behaviour.

As I aged, I outgrew most of my previous worries and learned to handle difficult situations with élan and confidence. But when it came to hair-stylists, I still had to watch my step, so to speak.

Jordanian hairdressers, irrespective of their gender, are breathtakingly beautiful. It is not necessarily a bad thing, but for men to be so good looking is, sort of, unfair.

I mean, other things remaining the same, it is more satisfying for a woman to be acknowledged for her natural beauty. Rather than a man, you know?

The first time I walked into a hairdressing salon in Amman, an Adonis lookalike turned to greet me with a dimpled smile. I felt my breathe getting stuck somewhere in my throat.

The initial moments of the interaction I can't recall very clearly now, but I found myself agreeing to whatever the hypnotic green gaze willed me to do. So, I sat through in a daze, as sections of my head were wrapped in silver foil paper and strong chemicals applied to it.

But when I heard the loud clicking of scissors, the spell was abruptly broken. My hairdresser had, by then, destroyed my tresses, which were lying in a careless heap, on the floor.

Out of an earlier childish habit, I reached up to instinctively cover my ears with my hands.

Adonis's twin stepped back, thinking I might punch him.

"You should have given in to the impulse," said the voice in my head.

Another empty threat?

Song Sung Blue

It is almost as if we live to sing.

It is hard to believe if you do not originate from a country like mine, but we have a song for every occasion: of love, sorrow, happiness, sadness, courtship, anger, jealousy, competitiveness, the list is exhaustive.

Our Bollywood movies might portray an exaggerated version of reality, but they are not far from the actual truth. Faced with any kind of predicament, we burst into song. And sometimes we sing for no particular reason at all.

Therefore, with so many singers around, nobody gives undue importance to this specific skill. We don't find it surprising to find people humming on the streets, into their telephones, through a bus window or even while taking a solitary walk. From over a million songs to pick from, there is never a dearth of choice, to suit any mood or temperament.

In fact, if somebody asks me, we should add this to our national description and call ourselves, the Secular Democratic Republic of Singing India. Nobody is really interested in taking my suggestion, but I'm offering it anyway.

Thus, you can be a good singer or a bad one but you can never be a non-singer. That is something, which is totally and completely unacceptable. In my homeland, nothing causes more alarm than admitting to this shortcoming. People look at you as if you have suddenly sprouted an extra head. It is easier to acknowledge being an alcoholic or a drug dealer, well nearly. Not that I have ever met such folks, but you know what I mean.

Our reputation in the international sphere also precedes us. About our so-called singing prowess, that is. In Jordan at least, you have to supply the proof of your Indian nationality in this manner. If you are unable to do so, they make you feel unpatriotic, somehow.

Stereotyping communities might be wrong, but that is exactly what all foreigners end up doing. Also, they supply an obscure lyric of any song, which they might remotely recall, and expect you to not only remember it, but also sing it to perfection.

I cannot even begin to tell you about where all I have been asked to sing. In the queue of an immigration counter, reception area of a tent hiring company, office of a refugee management NGO, and in front of a ticket window at Petra, among other places. I have become immune to random requests and nothing can surprise me any more. I have also prepared myself stoically, to be always ready with a song.

Quite unexpectedly, I became ill last week. The doctor said he needed to do some medical examinations under general anesthesia. I packed an overnighter and got myself admitted to the local hospital.

The nurses prepared me for surgery and discarded all the pretty nighties I had brought along. They dressed me in a light blue disposable gown and put me on a stretcher. As I was being wheeled into the operation theater, one male nurse asked me if I could sing for him.

"Which song?" I asked.

"Bol Radha Bol," he said.

"There is no such number," I mumbled.

"Sangam hoga ki nahin," he crooned.

"Nahin, kabhi nahin," I sang back automatically.

"What does it mean?" he wanted to know.

"Means, will Radha ever be yours?" I translated.

"She says yes?" he was hopeful.

"No, never," I laughed.

His crestfallen face was the last thing I remembered, before passing into oblivion.

What Women Want

If a gentle genie granted any woman three wishes, there is absolutely no telling what she might wish for.

A lot would depend upon what nature or nurture had already provided her with.

So, her random requests could range from the wellbeing of her family, a slender waistline, eradication of poverty, or a phone-call from her lover. In no particular order of preference, that is.

Does this mean that nobody really knows what a woman wants? Well, yes and no. In the sublime sense, there is no method in our perceived madness. But in practical terms, we definitely know what we desire.

In a nutshell, all we want is, to be happy.

It might seem like a Herculean task, trying to figure out precisely what makes us happy, but in fact it's quite easy, really. After the hullaballoo subsides, what stands out is one simple thing.

Women are happy when they are loved. And that is all.

It is not that we don't like being respected, admired or valued, we do. There is no doubt about that. But if there is one sentiment that can over-rule every other feeling, it is that of being loved. And in our heart of hearts we know that when we are loved, all the rest of it follows.

To give them this unconditional love, what do women look for in a partner? In order to discover this, I walked up to a group of cheerful ladies who were enjoying their coffee morning in a café, and decided to quiz them.

They were a quite uncommunicative to begin with, and did not like the idea of a stranger asking them intimate questions. But after some good-natured prodding, they decided to include me in the bonhomie. A frothy cappuccino was ordered, and the ice was broken, so to speak.

"What was the best quality that they admired in a man?" I asked.

"Intelligence and humour," they responded.

"But that is two traits," I protested.

"They go together," they said laughingly.

"Pick one," I insisted.

"In that case we would like to be with the person who makes us laugh," they claimed.

"What is the first thing you noticed in a gentleman?" I questioned.

Here everybody began speaking at once. They had so much to contribute that I had difficulty keeping up with them. The earlier restraint vanished as between giggles and mirthful shrieks, they shared confidences with me.

The answers ranged from the inane to the sublime: shoes, eyes, firm handshake, honesty, neatly trimmed fingernails, voice, kindness, courteousness, hair-cut, good manners and one even said *non-shifty gaze*!

After a few more confessions that are far too colourful to print I asked them to settle the issue, once and for all,

"What do women want?" I put across my query as gently as I could.

"To be loved happily ever after," they said, almost in unison.

I rest my case.

Driving Miss Daisy

I had heard horror stories about the infamous driving instructors of Jordan.

Every person I met in the first few weeks of relocating to the Hashemite Kingdom had a fresh take on it. Failing the examination, five to six times was normal, I was told. Managing to get a tutor to train you in the hot summer months when the schools were closed, was near impossible, I was informed.

Ah well, I said, preparing myself mentally for the long haul.

When in Rome, do as the Romans do.

This popular saying, by the way, originated in 387 AD and was first uttered by St. Ambrose. The story is that when St. Augustine arrived in Milan he noticed that the Church did not follow the same manner of worship on Saturdays, as it did in Rome. He complained to St. Ambrose, who was bishop of Milan. The wise man told him to follow the custom of the place wherever you are, and adapt accordingly.

Similarly, in order to mingle with the locals, I decided to do the compromising too. Meanwhile, I had one more problem. Not only were the driving instructors extremely busy, with every eighteen-year-old child training to become an ace driver, I had to also find one who could teach me in English. I was not proficient in Arabic and there was no way I could take instructions in an alien tongue.

The day of my first lesson dawned bright and sunny. The initial

booking was postponed by three hours, for reasons that were not considered important enough to be divulged to me.

My instructor was further delayed by thirty minutes, but having read about the unpredictability of Arabs, I was surprised that he actually showed up.

I was proud of being an excellent driver. I had maneuvered the car expertly around various metropolitan cities of the world and I wanted to showoff, on my very first attempt at driving in Jordan.

My instructor had other ideas.

Even before I put the car in gear, he cleared his throat and delivered a lengthy lecture.

"You are a woman," he said.

"Yes," I agreed.

"It is in your nature to be gentle. God made sure of that, so you should close the car doors softly," he continued without a pause.

"I will try my best," I promised.

"You must move the driving seat into a correct position tenderly, and adjust the rearview mirror lovingly," he told me.

"Of course," I agreed.

"Don't be in a hurry-hurry all the time. What for?" he questioned.

Not understanding the last query, I assumed he was asking why I needed to get a driving license.

"To be more independent," I said.

"Why do you need this independence, and why so fast-fast?" he quizzed.

"Sorry," I mumbled.

"Why you sorry?" he inquired immediately.

And in a similar vein, we continued.

I took fourteen-hour lessons in all. On the test day, I followed his directions to a 't', from closing the doors gently to adjusting the mirrors unhurriedly.

The result? What do you think?

Disciplinary Action

Parenting is a task like no other and there is an endless trial and error method associated with it.

There might be some broad guidelines to follow but every parent ends up drafting his or her own set of ground rules. They know that there is nothing more confusing for a child than to be faced with uncertain regulations. So they try to instill a sense of balance too.

In the old days *'Spare the rod and spoil the child'* was a saying that was taken quite literally. In school or at home, there existed an invisible line that was never crossed by the youngsters. There was always an authoritative figurehead who was summoned, as a warning, to frighten the hearts of children. In most houses the person to be afraid of was the father and in schools, it was the principal.

'Wait till the headmaster hears of this' was enough to make the bravest of my friends quiver in their boots. *'Let your dad get back from office'* had a similar effect too, especially on my brothers.

For a long time I wondered what actually would happen, because I never saw these threats being put into action. The admonition itself was sufficient in bringing all kinds of mischief, into an abrupt end.

But for the new generation, things changed. Children's rights groups decided that such disciplinary methods, did more harm than good, and passed a law to strictly ban it in future. Ironically, these days, to administer physical punishment has itself become a punishable offence.

So, when fear was removed as a tool for disciplining errant kids, the next concept that gained popularity involved reward as a motivation. Certain privileges could be granted or withheld according to the behaviour of the children and it was supposed to help in positive reinforcement. If followed strictly by the authoritarian figures, it worked wonders, and many youngsters discovered their true potential through this.

Whatever the manuals suggest, there are no foolproof techniques in disciplining kids. The only important thing is that if a method works, one must stick to it.

Through my own parenting years, the '*wait till your dad is here*' threat was always greeted by excited bouts of giggling by our child.

However much I tried, I could not instill fear by association with this warning, as she always looked forward to being in her father's presence. And so I devised a '*counting till three*' application.

Here I would count till the third numerical, and if our daughter did not perform a given task by that time, a promised book or treat would be taken away. I had to painstakingly train her, day in and day out. For my pains, till eternity I have been labeled as the stricter parent.

One day I came home to see my husband mimicking my disciplinary mannerisms. Our kid was placed on a high chair at the dining table.

She was staring rebelliously at the food on her plate. My spouse was trying to persuade her to eat.

Imitating me, he started to count.

"One," he said.

There was no reaction.

"Two," he recited.

Still nothing.

"Two and a half?" he suggested.

Peals of instantaneous laughter followed. In the twinkling of an eye, he spooned baby food, into her open mouth.

Ah well, you win some!

Bag Lady

Society ladies can be classified into two broad categories: the ones who love shoes, and those that are partial to handbags.

Occasionally, there might be a woman who likes to collect both. But mostly, it is one or the other that we go shopping for.

I am a bag lady.

Whether it is a purse, tote, clutch or pouch I love them all. In fact, I like backpacks, knapsacks, carryalls and shoulder-slings too. Wallets, billfold frames, briefcases and attachés also attract my attention.

Even when I'm in a mad rush, it is impossible for me to walk past a shop window that exhibits handbags. I somehow find myself lingering and admiring the handiwork on display. It is just a weird compulsion that I cannot explain.

I have noticed that the salespeople in any handbag store are the friendliest folks on the planet. They entice you with charming smiles, and before you know it, you are queuing up in the purchasing line.

Moreover, what is admirable about a handbag-carrying lady is what she manages to stuff into it. It is supposed to hold a few indispensable items like house-keys, cash, credit-cards and cell-phone. But what it ends up with is a truckload of essential knickknacks.

Let me tell you about a few of the things that can be found in it. Sunglasses, spectacles, lipstick, lip balm, pack of tissues, hand

sanitizer, driving-license, tablets for headache, motion sickness or allergies, chewing-gum, rolls of mint, ATM card, medical insurance card, business cards of people you have met, ballpoint pen, pictures of your children and a small notepad, at the very least.

While traveling, our passports, valuable jewels and tickets also get transported there. And depending on the stage of our lives, from kid's pacifiers to spouse's hearing aides; we cart all of that, too.

It is no wonder that with lugging such a large burden at all times, we periodically suffer from tennis elbow or frozen shoulder. The orthopedic specialists first inspect the weight of our handbag even before they examine our inflamed and painful joints.

Part of the prescription is painkilling medication, of course. But more important is the suggestion to reduce the load in our purses.

Last week I accompanied a group of visitors on a sight seeing trip. Warning the ladies about the long walk inside Petra, I cautioned them against carrying heavy handbags. They unhappily discarded a few non-vital items.

But Mary didn't. She hauled an entire knapsack on her lap and kept it there for the entire journey.

Within the first few minutes, someone complained of thirst. Mary quickly pulled out a water bottle from her bag. At the midway point, she passed around chips, biscuits, sugar-free sweeteners and mosquito repellants. All this came out of her handbag.

In Petra, battery operated hand-fans, energy laced drinks, and flat walking-shoes were handed out. After a moment, folded umbrellas, sun-block lotions and scented towels were distributed. Next, traveler's guide, dried nuts, and whatever she or any of her companions needed, was instantly produced, from within the confines of her handbag.

Since that remarkable trip, I have now passed on the label.

Mary is now the new bag lady!

Memory Bank

Some people are blessed with a phenomenal art of recollection. They never admit to it, because that leads to an unflattering comparison of having the memory of an elephant. These intelligent mammals, though gentle and benign, are not terribly complimentary to be associated with.

So, they withhold this information voluntarily but keep storing tidbits in their brain. When the time comes for recall, they manage to recollect everything, even the minutest of facts, to recreate a past incident in all its photographic detail.

My memory used to be pretty good too.

While relating a conversation, for instance, I could remember small particulars like, the colour of a dress the person was wearing, or the brightness of his tiepin. If there was a slight nasal inflection in the voice; or a trivial lisp in the speech; crookedness of tooth; or crinkling of eyes; it would all get recorded subconsciously in my head.

My listeners were greatly surprised and would later ask me how I could remember the scenes so precisely, but I just shrugged and took this innate skill for granted.

However, as time passed, I began to bungle up. First I started mixing the names. I would meet a person, be formally introduced to them, and in the next five minutes itself go blank. For the rest of the evening I either avoided calling out to them or, in some embarrassing occasions, called them by the wrong name.

Then, I started to make a mishmash of all the other aspects

also. I would overlook the specifics of where we met, or when an incident had taken place. Also, while reminiscing about anything, I would forget what I was saying, right in the middle of a tale.

Scared at this sudden complication, I decided to delve into self-help books. I liked a particular one that taught 'memory by association'.

In this exercise, I had to associate whatever I needed to remember, with some image or location. Using hyperbole to exaggerate a scene was encouraged and we could embellish the scenario to make the image seem bigger, bolder, or funnier. Mentally, that is.

I thought I would put it to immediate use.

So, to memorize the timing of my impending flight at two in the afternoon, I pictured an airplane. The aircraft had two wings; therefore I imagined them flapping birdlike, both of them. I was surprised how easily I managed to commit this to memory. It worked smoothly and I was in the airport well on time.

At the next social occasion I was prepared. As soon as I met Sam Fields, I scrutinised his face carefully. He had the most amazingly bushy eyebrows, which stood out prominently, right on top of his twinkling eyes.

I used creative association to nail down his name. I visualised the hair from his thick brows floating in a field of yellow corn. Pleased with myself, I called out to him at several instances during the course of the evening. Each time I was absolutely accurate.

Just before leaving for home, I went to say goodbye.

"Now, don't forget his name," said the voice in my head.

"Won't you introduce us?" asked my spouse.

"Meet Mister Eyebrow Fields," I said instinctively.

"Interesting name," my husband chuckled.

"Very interesting," the host laughed.

"Well, gentlemen, there is this book…," I tried to explain, but no one was listening.

Fortunes of a Cookie

My problem is that I am a skeptic.
If there is talk of any predictions, horoscopes, or conjectures, I am the first to denounce it.

Even though the forecasters tried to shrivel me with their contemptuous looks, I have laughed outright at the prophesies of gloom and doom. Despite their scorn, I find it impossible to believe in any kind of claptrap.

But last week something caught my attention. I had just taken the first sip of my favourite brew when I noticed that the teabag, which was dipped into my cup, had a note on it. Pulling out the attached string, I peered at the cardboard cutout.

'*Disbelief destroys the magic!*' I read. "Sure, but you have to first create it," said the voice in my head.

During dinner at a corner Chinese restaurant the same evening, I was presented with a plateful of fortune cookies. I picked up a handful and got them home. I had no idea what these triangular brown crispy things were.

Researching on the Internet I discovered, to my complete surprise, that though they were sold in Chinese stores, they had not originated in China. In fact, nobody had even heard of them there. Various theories pointed to San Francisco, or Los Angeles as the places where they were invented. In the early part of the 20th century, that is.

Shaped like a horseshoe, these sweet cookies contained thin

pieces of paper, with words of wisdom printed on them. The predictions were revealed after cracking them open and that is why they were called '*fortune cookies*'.

Once I got home, I dumped the packet, with my car keys. The next morning I saw them discarded carelessly on my office desk. Before I could stop myself, I opened the first one and gently extracted a piece of paper from inside.

'*Congratulations! You are on your way!*' it announced. I was on my way? But where was I heading? O how I hated these cryptic clues!

'*Dedicate yourself with a calm mind to the task at hand!*' cautioned the second fortune cookie.

I almost dropped the crumpled bits on the floor. What was happening? I was neglecting my work, but how did the Chinese wafer know that?

I gazed over my shoulder to see if anyone was standing there. Maybe, somebody was watching me on CCTV and supplying all the information to the cookie-prediction-writer. Who could tell? I took one more careful look around, but noticed nothing unusual.

I decided to ignore the rest of the cookies and get started on my assignment. Must be sheer coincidence, I said to myself. I dismissed the entire thing, and for the next several moments worked in silence.

The last two cookies were still in front of me. From the corner of my eye I saw them, perched provocatively on my table. Let me check both and get it over and done with, I decided.

'*You are working hard*' suggested the third biscuit. Before I could fully digest this, I cracked the final one.

'*You must stand up to be seen, speak up to be heard and shut upto be appreciated*!' it said.

Well chastened, I am now a silent believer of cookie magic.

The Vanishing Breed

Not so long ago, the interaction between patients and doctors was simple.

The moment you felt unwell, you went to a doctor. In fact, it was simpler than that too. If you fell sick, you just sent for one.

The specialist would arrive, holding a stethoscope in one hand, and a square-shaped medical case in the other. Without fail, all of them would present themselves in this identical manner.

A member of the family would receive him or her at the door, and most respectfully, taking over the heavy bag, escort them to the patient's bedside.

These doctors were GPs or General Practitioners and there was nothing rushed about them. When they came to do the check-ups, they had a calm bedside manner. Irrespective of whether you were suffering from a stomach ache or back trouble, the medical examination was the same.

First, you had to stick your tongue out, which was checked for its right shade of pinkness. Next, a guttural sound had to be emitted while your throat was inspected. The eyelids were peeled back, and the exact colour tested.

The stethoscope would be pressed on the chest and back. The stomach rapped with sharp knuckles, and the knees gently tapped with a tiny hammer like instrument.

All this was done even before the pulse was counted or the rise in body temperature marked. These would be documented, and the blood pressure recorded. And only then, a measured and unhurried diagnosis was made.

These GPs were, and behaved like, old family friends. They knew the background of the patients from infancy, and were aware of all their allergies and former ailments. They prescribed the medication according to this past medical history.

Sometimes, they would declare that there was nothing wrong with the sick person, and all that was needed, was some fresh air, and bland food.

The families took these suggestions, and followed the instructions meticulously, with positive results showing within a few days.

The thought of doubting these doctors never crossed their minds. In very rare instances, if appendicitis or heart trouble were suspected, they would recommend an appropriate surgeon to the concerned family, and even escort them to the hospital.

Sadly, these days the GPs are a vanishing breed. With the speed with which modern science has advanced, medical profession now has doctors who are super-specialists. In the field of ophthalmology, for instance, there are specialists in retinal therapy, experts in lens correction, and others who treat glaucoma cases. At one level it is wonderful to have so many options, but on the other hand, it is terribly confusing.

I was reminiscing about this when I fell sick recently during a vacation. A hotel room is a terrible place to be ill in, especially when you are on a jungle safari. The resort staff offered to call a medical practitioner, who was the local GP.

Soon the elderly doctor arrived. My husband received him at the door. They spent the first five minutes catching up on world politics and discussing the weather. He then approached my bedside. My spouse was carrying his square medical bag.

"Let me check your tongue young lady," instructed the doctor.

Next, he pulled down my eyelids.

I knew I was in safe hands, and by evening I was as good as new.

Wag the Dog

You don't have to examine them closely in order to notice the similarity.

One casual glance is enough to confirm the obvious fact that pet-owners and their pets resemble one another in an uncanny, unbelievable and unexplainable sort of way.

I did not give much credence to this idea initially.

But recently I came across a photograph. It was of a golden retriever pup grinning wolfishly at the camera. The picture was taken ten or fifteen years back, and for a moment I could not pinpoint who the snapshot reminded me of.

Then, all of a sudden, it came to me in a flash. The happy puppy looked exactly like an unruly version of me. In a much younger, untidier form but our dark eyes, rakish smile, and unkempt hair looked identical.

I never spotted this while he was alive. There was just no time for any kind of philosophical introspection then, as he kept me extremely busy.

I could not prepare for his arrival because we adopted him on a whim, with no prior planning. He was a tiny, few weeks old, chocolate coloured bundle when I picked him up for the first time. He curled into my palm and clung to my shoulder refusing to let go. I had to bring him home.

When I gave him a bath, all the dirt accumulated on his little body washed off, and he emerged as a light cream, fluffy ball.

We called him Zar and he was an absolute delight.

When he was small, his favourite mode of travel was my lap. He loved attention, and curious children stopped me in public places to ask, if they could cuddle him.

As he became bigger I had to start the tough job of house training him. Many nights he would wake me up with a false whine, and when I took him out into the garden to do his business, he would go on an unending sniffing trail.

If I rushed him, he would come back indoors, and promptly piddle on the leg of my expensive sofa.

Doggy biscuits were what he lived for. I could make him do anything, if the reward was a crunchy cookie. When he grew older his body became stronger. Very soon he started resembling a huge, gigantic lion. He was supposed to be our guard dog, but was the friendliest mutt alive, and was more capable of jumping on a stranger and slobbering him with drool rather than biting him to death.

Everything scared him, including the sound of his own bark. His greatest pastime was chasing cats, but if a particular vicious one hissed at him, he would come scurrying, to hide behind my back. From that safe position he would continue to snarl at them.

Zar spent every moment of his life around me. So when he contacted leukemia, I had to make one of the most agonizing decisions I have ever made.

The vet suggested that this was the kindest thing we could do and it was time to let him go.

The melting brown eyes looked at me in complete trust, as I held him in my lap, for one last time. The injection was painless and within minutes it halted his laboured breathing.

His loss was devastating and I have still not completely recovered from it.

The belated realisation that I resembled my dog is like a balm to my grieving soul.

Bedside Story

A good night's sleep is a Godsend; there is no denying that. In babyhood, teenage years and early youth all you had to do was shut your eyes. The posture did not matter, the noise in the vicinity was immaterial, the bed, cot, sofa, bench, firm ground, any flat surface in fact, was considered suitable for lulling you to sound sleep.

But somewhere along the way, niggling backache made its presence felt and the mattress I was sleeping on was pinpointed as a possible culprit. Its softness or hardness was supposed to be the cause of the pain. This, in turn, was responsible for the interruption in my sleeping pattern.

And so I started exploring mattresses, and what started off as natural curiosity, quickly turned into a full-fledged investigation. The sheer variety of the available product had my head reeling. From spring to foam, water to air, the list was endless. There were also subdivisions to these, and further super specialisations to those, too.

The names, incidentally, were exceedingly alluring. The four basic types were called: open spring-where the arrangement was in rows and connected with a thick spiral wire; pocket spring-which was housed in individual cloth partitions, allowing them to work independently; latex foam – which sprang back to its original shape when you got up, and memory foam – which did not retain its original form but maintained an imprint of your body contour.

Also, there were mattress toppers. What is that, you ask? It is, as the term suggests, exactly like a layer of extra toppings on a pizza. Only, here it did not enhance taste, but was used as an additional covering for the mattress. Some of these were down feather ones, made from the soft plume of geese or ducks; others were wool toppers that were resistant to bed bugs but manufactured from lamb's fleece and the rest were egg crate toppers that literally looked like a large but empty tray of eggs.

As if all of this was not confusing enough, any query about a mattress, first required the buyer to fill out a quiz-form that had inquisitive questions like, do you sleep on your back, side or stomach? Do you toss and turn around in your sleep?

And then it got more personal. Do you get excessively hot or cold while sleeping? Does your partner move around in the bed and wake you up? I mean, why delve into such intricate details about a person's life that they themselves were clueless about?

There were even suggestions for free. Like, take your pillow along when you go shopping for a mattress.

"What would the shopkeeper think?" said the voice in my head. If the thought itself were scandalizing me, how would a stranger react?

I got to know soon enough. My disturbed sleep had me running to the nearest mattress shop. Concealed discretely, in an enormous shopping basket, was my favourite pillow.

"Good morning Ma'am, how are you today?" the salesman's voice boomed at me.

"Fine," I smiled.

"You want to buy a mattress?" he asked.

"Yes," my husband replied.

"You are together?" he inquired.

We nodded in response.

"Ok, in which position do you sleep?" he queried.

"I sleep on my back, he sleeps on his side," I said.

"She sleeps on her side, I sleep on my back," spouse responded.

"Are you married?" he probed exasperatedly.

"To each other," we chorused.

"So let's do trial by pillow," he announced taking over my big bag.

Aunt Horror

It was not easy to hide from them because they had an invisible third eye, at the back of their heads.

Nothing escaped their attention either, and no amount of training could make them mind their own business.

They were bold creatures, fearless and brave. Every family had them in large numbers, and without asking or even praying for it, I was blessed with a truckload too. Over the years, I developed a bitter-sweet relationship with them.

Who were these mysterious individuals? A strong contingent of unsung ladies related to us by heredity, genes, or pure coincidence, they were our Aunties and dear Lord! You could love them, or hate them, but try as you might, you couldn't disown them.

Dad's and mom's sisters, parents' brothers' wives, their cousins, cousins of cousins, once or twice removed, even three times removed, all came collectively clubbed under one giant-sized umbrella that spelt, *Aunt*, in neon letters.

These women were divided into two broad categories: strict and stricter. They frowned over everything that you did. Or didn't do. Difficult to please, they started their sentences with 'don't mind my saying this' and then proceeded to tell you things that shattered your self-esteem to its very core.

When I was younger, most of their advice to me was contradictory. So, if I was thin, I was told to eat more, but make sure I did not become obese. If forgot to exercise, I was made to

start swimming immediately, but not get sunburnt because then no one would want to marry me.

What the connection was between sunburn and lack of matrimonial alliance was never explained.

But as I grew older, I perfected a trick, and the moment I saw one of them approaching, after the perfunctory hello, I feigned illness, and disappeared.

According to them, their own children were better than my siblings and me, in everything, whether it was academics or sports. Albeit untrue, we were not allowed to argue with them. It was considered impolite, so we had to just grin and bear it.

And then before I knew it, I became an Aunt myself. Suddenly I had four nephews in my basket. Being the only sister to my brothers and brothers-in-law, I was also their solitary Aunty. It was a responsible role and these little chaps looked up to me. I decided to spoil them rotten from day one. I mean, what did I have to lose?

So, we had wolf whistling competitions, spitting on the furthest step contest, marble-slingshot challenges, and imaginary guns and robbers games, devised by me. I was their chief confidant, storyteller, barber and also the person with a nonstop supply of petty cash.

My only caveat was that if anybody asked them how many Aunts they had, the reply had to be '*one*' with a smart salute executed towards me. I painstakingly trained them to do this, and they performed it perfectly.

Once a little one came running towards me and asked for a chocolate treat. His mum shook her head because it would have ruined his appetite for dinner. I was caught in a quandary.

"I have to tell you something," he lisped, tugging at my arm.

"Yes darling," I said, picking him up.

"Do you know how many Aunties I have?" he asked.

"One?" I prompted, smiling broadly.

"None!" he whispered furiously, before running off.

Boys will be boys.

The Book Collector

Story telling is one of the oldest surviving art forms.
It can be polished, for sure. Addition of musical notes and dance steps embellish and enhance its narrative, uplifting it further. That is how it continues to thrive.

There are stories that we hear one moment and promptly forget in the next. But there are also those that we have heard repeatedly, and wish to hear, all over again. These tales have taken the form of epics, legends, and mythologies. The ultimate test of a good story is its resilience, and enduring quality.

Psychologists divide everyone into visual or audio learner groups. But observing a crowd of rapt toddlers around an animated storyteller, I am convinced that the method, in which certain stories are read out, is what makes them popular. To the young children, that is.

However as they grow older, most bookworms like to do the reading by themselves. The problem, for voracious readers is in controlling the inflow of books into their lives. The collection expands at such an alarming pace that sometimes, the rooms in their house start to resemble a library. When the heap becomes too huge to handle, one has to learn to exercise restraint.

I love books, and at the slightest excuse I run to a bookstore. When a new one opened in my city, I hurried there on the first day itself. The visual display was very tempting with an array of new titles enticing me. But remembering the mountain of books on two sides of my bed I wanted to go easy.

As I made my way to the checkout area, I gave myself a few minutes to make up my mind, and discard at least two volumes from the huge stack that I had selected. But any book that I tried to abandon silently pleaded with me to buy it. You might think I'm exaggerating but this is exactly what was happening.

The lady at the cash counter was losing patience with me. Imagine the scene. I would hand her one book to be scanned for payment through the till machine. As soon as the cash register rang, I would take the book back, and ask her to cancel the order. The next book would be tentatively passed, while keeping the first one tightly clasped in my other hand.

We continued in this manner for a while, till she started to look completely exasperated. I even thought of placing a short call to my husband. Maybe he could help me in the final selection.

Eventually, we came to a compromise. No, not the sales lady and me; she had long given up and passed me on to an older, more patient looking clerk. I yielded to the tussle over the book choices, and surrendered to myself. In an instantaneous snap decision, I decided to buy all twenty of them.

"Shall I start charging for the books Ma'am?" asked the elderly salesman.

"Yes," I said, beaming at him.

"You want to return some of them now, right?" he suggested.

"No," I replied.

"You want to recalculate?" he probed kindly.

"No" I repeated.

"How many do you want to buy?" he quizzed.

"All of them," I told him.

"A librarian, are you?" he eyed me suspiciously.

"You could say that," I answered, hiding my smile and picking up the heavy shopping bag.

In Search of Excellence

We pass this angst to our kids at some point in their nurturing. I wish that we didn't. But we have an innate desire to prove to our children that when we were younger, things were better. And so we exaggerate about our own childhood.

It is not easy being on the other side of the fence, especially if you have been an awfully hyper, and demanding child yourself. Progressing from there, to the stage of becoming a seriously responsible parent is all the more difficult. You have to just keep trying.

It is very humbling too, as at every drawback, you have to restart, and continue with the exercise. Of becoming exemplary role models, that is.

But what most of us dread is the ultimate nightmare of failing to live up to our child's expectations and losing the halo that they place around our heads. No, we don't need to be put on a pedestal as parents, but there is no need to expose our feet of clay, either.

So, we reminisce. We look back at our own childhood. We edit all the negatives and through rose-filtered glasses, paint a glossier picture for our offspring. We tell them that when we were children, things were so much better.

And then we get carried away. We tell them that things were not only better, they were also: simpler, healthier, purer, funnier and we encapsulate our entire upbringing as some sort of a utopian ideal, which can never be recreated.

There is not much truth to this bragging; we realise that in our saner moments. But we basically continue the tradition, and dole out to our children, what our parents doled out to us. It is called the circle of life.

However, sometimes we are forced to face facts. The other day our daughter was on a quizzing spree.

"Did you have e-mail when you were little, Mom?" she asked.

"No, but we used to write in longhand, beautiful letters penned in ink," I told her.

"You mean no Internet too? How did you research your projects?" she was shocked.

"Well, we had the encyclopedia, an entire collection of it," I boasted.

"But you had the television, right?" she went on.

"Nope! TV came to our town when I was in high school. It had only one channel, which was run by the government. They broadcasted the news in English and then in the regional language with something called '*spot the farmer*' that had tips on methods and modes of farming," I informed her happily.

"Are you saying you could not watch movies at home?" she wanted to know.

"Of course not! Films were screened in the clubs where the spools made a hissing sound intermittently. We loved those movie nights by the pool side," I gushed.

"No computers, no cell phones, no DVD, CD, iPods, no music systems too? And you say you had a great upbringing? Mum, you poor thing, what did you do with your time?" she sympathised.

"But we were busy all day," I declared.

"Doing what?" she asked, losing interest in my glittering past.

"Must be something, got to be, I will cook up something," I rambled to her retreating back.

Pearls of Wisdom

As I entered the plush interiors of a dental clinic in Amman, the first thing that caught my eye was an impressive poster.

A stunning woman, her profile captured in close-up, looked down from the wall. Her teeth were gleaming, in perfect whiteness.

The slogan read, '*Smile! It improves your face value*'.

"Sure," said the voice in my head. If only I had a mouthful of pearly whites to show off. With a weakness for sweets, chocolates and éclairs of the sticky variety, the resultant disaster was imprinted in the fillings lining the length and breadth of my jaw. Having a sweet tooth was bad enough, but learning to live with an entire set of sweet teeth was what made smiling, an extremely painful exercise for me.

All of this flitted through my mind as I waited in the lounge adjoining the dentist's chambers.

Suddenly, the heavy doors opened, and before the receptionist could announce his arrival, the dentist strode out purposefully, and escorted me to his den.

What struck me about his appearance was his height, or rather, the lack of it. Seated on his high chair, behind a heavy desk, he looked tall enough. But the moment he abandoned that posture, he measured about five feet, in his flat shoes.

It was this petite frame that gave him the added advantage of looking vulnerable, a fact that allowed his patients to trust him, more than they should have. He did not believe in curing you of just an aching tooth. He preached the practice of a brand new orthodontic lifestyle.

So, he started his lecture, with a vigorous demonstration on how to wield a toothbrush. This was followed by a lengthy discourse on what kind of tools to buy, for meticulous dental hygiene.

Making a total mockery of the way most of us brushed our teeth, from side to side, he promoted the brush strokes go up and down to massage the gums. After imprinting this set of cardinal rules in my head, he approached the problem with another equally firm belief, that elimination was better than cure.

So, I was persuaded to have my cavity-ridden molar extracted on the very first visit to his clinic. It was half unhinged, and was causing me immense pain. The second trip had me agreeing to the removal of another tooth, which according to the good doctor, was growing outwards.

It could cut the inside of my jaw, leading to cheek cancer, he warned me. I quickly consented to the uprooting, not wishing to contradict his wise suggestions. And came home, minus one more errant tooth.

On the following visit, I parted company with yet another of my wisdom teeth totally brainwashed into believing that it was crucial for me to get a gold cap.

By now my husband saw through the whole scam.

"What is wrong with you?" he asked me.

"The dentist said that it was what I urgently needed," I explained.

"A dozen or more such visits and you will need a brand new set of perfect dentures," he joked.

"But my teeth had cavities in them," I protested.

"It is better to have some teeth, albeit cavity ridden, than to have no teeth at all," he warned.

Though belated, it made complete sense to me. Three painful dental visits, and three missing teeth later, I am now a wise woman.

The Pursuit of Happiness

'*When you are happy and you know it clap your hands.*'
The simple words of this nursery rhyme tries to teach us, in kindergarten itself, how to show happiness. But the all-important question is, how to be happy? What does one do to attain happiness and where is contentment found?

These are modest queries, but unfortunately, there are no straightforward answers to them.

It has plagued philosophers, psychologists and sociologists since time immemorial. Countries all over the world, conduct surveys to measure the happiness indices of its population. Also, the responses-here I'm hoping that all the respondents are truthful-are stupefying.

For instance: riches and affluence do not count where being happy is concerned. The basic bare minimum of wealth, is supposed to help. If you do not have even a roof over your head, or three square meals to eat, and still claim to be happy then you are obviously lying. But once these essential needs are met, further accumulation of material goods will not make you happier.

So, what will? Increase your happiness quotient, that is.

A new study issued by a popular iPhone application, showed that Jordan was amongst the least happy countries in the world. It ranked ninety-second on a list of a hundred and twenty four nations that were surveyed.

Why were the people of my resident country so unhappy? I decided to ask around.

My chemist down the lane confessed that she was reasonably cheerful. Her job was okay, but she was looking forward to the day when her three daughters would graduate from college.

"Getting them well educated is what makes me happy, and once they are settled in their careers, I will find nice husbands for them, God willing!" she told me.

The waiter at a local restaurant said he was content with his life in Amman, but he was happiest when he received a letter from his home in Philippines.

"My wife and children are always on my mind. When I know that they are well, I feel fine," he said.

The teenager I met in the ice-cream parlour confided that he was only happy when he zipped around in his car, racing with his friends every weekend.

"And when I win the race, which I do every now and then, I am very happy," he laughed.

At a movie theatre, I noticed a lady who was surreptitiously wiping tears while watching an emotional drama on screen. I was curious to hear her response because she looked upset.

"I love tragic films. I get very involved in the plot, with all its despair. The heartbreaking scenes make me cry but I am very happy with all the sadness," she smiled and sniffled at the same time.

Getting such diverse answers got me worried because I could not reach any definitive conclusion. My notes read: welfare of family, pursuing a hobby and cathartic misery.

While still pondering on this, I glanced out of the window and saw a bright sun in the sky. After two days of incessant rain, the clear sunshine lit up my garden, gloriously. The flowers that I had planted swayed gently in the breeze. The sight was simply magnificent.

A sense of happiness filled my heart, and I fought a sudden urge to clap my hands.

Friend Indeed

Here is a scenario.

Imagine, in your mind's eye: two women friends reuniting after a gap of few months. They squeal in delight, hugging and smothering each other in affection. For the next several hours they are inseparable, as they talk nonstop in a chatter laced with generous compliments.

Now visualise another scene: two men friends meeting up after a substantial span of time. The initial hug later, they slap one another on the shoulders. And then, grinning broadly, the insults start pouring, fast and furious, with no holding back.

Real life is exactly like these two contrasting situations. Females demonstrate love towards the members of their tribe with sweet words, and males, by sour ones.

For a long while I could not comprehend this disparity. When I was newly married and not accustomed to my brand new husband's mannerisms, I would be horrified with this kind of behavior. Especially when I met his best buddy for the first time.

These two gentlemen were extremely close, or that is what I was made to understand. They had a shared childhood, went to the same schools, colleges and got in and out of innumerable scrapes together. From drinking binges, bunking classes to motorcycle races, there was hardly any escapade they had not done jointly. I had to lend a patient hearing to all the detailed description, whenever the chap's name came up.

So, I was told about the time they had swiped comics to make a children's lending library, where the kids had to borrow their own pilfered magazines back, for a small fee. My husband would laugh uproariously while relating this specific story. It was all his idea, he confessed, and they thought it would collapse in a week's time. But surprisingly, it lasted for six whole months, before an angry mother came after them with a rolling pin.

Their unbeatable score in one particular cricket match; the unanimous support during a college election campaign and the crazy party they had after the win; when they got drunk on cheap beer and were laid-up in bed for a week afterwards; the double dates, the mountain climbing fiasco, the cigarette smoking experiments, the rustling of instant noodles at midnight; everything was related to me in bits and pieces.

Having heard so much about this individual, I was really looking forward to meeting him in person. He had relocated to America so I had to wait till we travelled to that part of the world. My husband wanted to surprise him, so he did not call his friend till we touched down in San Francisco.

But, once there, the bloke refused to meet us. He had apparently worn a thick beard all through his youth, and had shaved it off just that week. The new look did not suit him, he claimed. So he did not want to face us with this unfamiliar appearance.

My spouse would not have any of it. He put us into a taxicab and we landed up at his doorstep.

"Hey Man! You made it!" his friend said, enveloping us in a warm hug.

"Sure! But how did you become bald?" my husband responded, smiling.

"And you finally developed a paunch, Fatty?" he asked.

"Who is Fatty?" I wanted to know.

"You haven't told her? Till now?" he queried.

"Don't believe anything this rogue says," spouse cautioned.

"Come with me, I will enlighten you about this scoundrel," he insisted.

Friends indeed?

Complimenting Issues

There is something about the fairer sex that is averse to compliments.

We do like them make no mistake. It is foolish to suggest, even in jest, that we dislike paeans sung in our honour. We love everything to do with it: the gushing admiration, the undivided attention, and so on. Yet, the fact remains that we do not know how to graciously accept praise. The trouble is that we view it as a puzzle, and a cryptic one at that.

Therefore, if someone says that's a lovely coat you are wearing, to a woman, her response is either, 'Oh, this old thing? I bought it four years back at a garage sale', or, 'But you should see how great it looks on my sister'. It might even be, 'You know, it actually has a torn pocket which I have hidden with my handbag'.

These, and many such nonsensical explanations, generally follow a simple compliment. So much so that the person doing the admiring moves away in bemusement.

All of this can be easily avoided if we smile in response and say 'thank you'. That's it, nothing more, nothing less.

But we cannot beam in gratitude because that might imply an end to the tête-à-tête. We are terrible at ending conversations everyone knows that. Also, it would mean that we have accepted the generous remark and are, perhaps, worthy of it.

That is our biggest problem because we are poor acceptors, and as soon as we receive something unexpectedly, we start to justify

it. Thus, we go off at a tangent and complicate the issue by offering inane and irrational validations, to the compliment giver.

There is no need to do any of this. But who can drill sense into our stubborn heads? We are, by the very nature of our gender, so insecure about our goodness, that we cannot handle acclaim objectively.

I wish there was some way to inculcate in us a suitable etiquette of receiving compliments: like a precise manner in which to nod our heads or murmur our responses. It would do us a world of good.

When nobody stepped up to guide me, I decided to train my own self. I would, for one entire week, acknowledge all the compliments that came my way with dignified gratitude, I decided. I would if I could, become an ideal compliment receiver, without offering any explanations or justifications for them.

Unfortunately, the first five days of my experimental week went without compliments. Nobody, even remotely or in a flippant manner, complimented me.

But on the sixth day, I was rewarded, so to speak. Busy weeding the bushes in my garden, I saw a head appear around the front gate. It belonged to a complete stranger, but she had the friendliest smile on her face.

"You have planted gorgeous flowers," she gushed.

"Thank you," I smiled in response.

There was a lull in the exchange, as I did not supply anything after that.

"I love your gardening gloves," my would-be friend tried, one more time.

"Thank you," I smiled, again.

We eyed each other uncertainly in the accompanying silence, and then she turned around, and walked off.

I got a sinking feeling that I lost a friend, even before I made one.

Recycling Methods

❖

One must admit that gifts come in very good packaging these days, with glossy shiny paper, which is sometimes transparent, and the bows tied in satiny ribbons that trail in all direction.

It can be quite intimidating too and at times it is better to view the present from a safe distance, than actually unwrap it. "Why spoil the artistically packaged creation?" says the voice in the head.

I come from a country of recyclers. Much before it became a global phenomenon, with enthusiastic individuals campaigning for its awareness, Indians were recycling everything. Large tomato sauce bottles, when emptied, were washed and put out in the sun to dry. They were then used for storing drinking water.

In the town where I spent my childhood, there was hardly any household that did not have these bottles in their refrigerator. In fact some of them still carried a sticker of the squash or lemonade that it originally contained. People would try scrubbing it off with an iron scrubber but give up midway, if the glue was strong.

Old sarees were converted into curtains or tablecloths and older sarees were used as a stuffing while making quilts. Newspapers lined not only the kitchen and bathroom shelves but were also reused for wrapping gifts. It made for quite a sober sight and no child was overtly excited with a toy packed inside a cover that announced robberies, murders or election results under its headlines.

The gifts themselves were boringly practical. I mean why would a five year old boy be happy with a one meter shirt length piece of cloth as a birthday present? Or even a token twenty-one bucks, hastily put inside an envelope? There would always be that additional one coin for extra goodwill.

So, the denominations ranged between a very tight fisted eleven, gifted by miserly relatives, to an extremely generous one hundred and one, presented by extravagant friends. It did not make the children happy, because they hardly had any use for money. But it put a smile on the faces of their parents, for sure.

What delighted us were the gift boxes, literally too. For instance, if there were a watch or a pen-set that was presented, we kids would pounce on the empty containers. The unusual shapes of the cartons would fire our imagination. We created games around these make-believe tankers or tunnels and it kept us busy for hours on end. We used them to keep our glass marbles, especially if the cardboard case was elongated.

Foreign products were not easily available those days and an empty coke can occupied a pride of place in my study table. It doubled up as a stationary holder with thin pencils popping out of it. The joy was in collecting these rare bits and pieces and reusing them.

But the youngsters today are completely immune to these self-innovation techniques. Recently we received a massive gift of flowers. I immediately started to rearrange the bouquet.

"She will put the bigger flowers in big vases," my spouse announced.

"And dry the smaller ones for potpourri," our daughter added.

"Paint the flower pot too," my husband predicted.

"In black and gold maybe," guessed the little one.

"You forgot the satin ribbon and the cellophane paper," I reminded.

"Iron the first and fold the second," they instructed.

"And this sponge?" I held up the soaked square.

"Will hit one of our heads if we don't shut up," they chorused.

Wake-up with Make-up

Like *Rebecca*, the exotic heroine of Daphne Du Maurier's story, 'last night I dreamt I went to Manderley again'.

I must confess though, that I have never seen the rambling estate with its palatial villa called Manderley, which was brilliantly brought alive in fiction. But I did visit a monument in Cyprus where the author stayed for ten months while writing her novel.

Of all things from the bygone era, what I miss most is the fuss that ladies made with their elaborate dressing-up ritual.

Men dressed up formally too, for dinner parties, extravagant weddings and also, while traveling. See any black and white pictures of people emerging from an airplane and notice how immaculately clad they all were, about forty years back. A far cry from the tracksuit, and faded jeans clothed untidy passengers of today.

Going overseas on a steamer-ship or by air was dignified business and the travelers took the trouble of turning up in their best clothes for the occasion. Women wore smartly tailored dresses, accessorised with elegant jewels. Men, almost all of them, sported dark suits and polished shoes.

A decorum was maintained with no pushing or shoving between the queues and people, arriving after several days of travel, looked perfectly spruced up, and fresh as daisies.

When I was little I loved seeing my mother and other women getting ready for parties. I watched in fascination as they expertly applied their make-up that subtly transformed them into ultra

glamorous divas. Each of them had a dressing table with a huge mirror, in front of which they sat, on a cushioned chair.

My favourite Aunt used to notice me standing by her side, and would flick a perfumed feather like powder-puff on my cheeks. A thin coat of the glittering dust sprinkled on my face, and I would refuse to wash it off for the rest of the evening.

I also carefully observed the tricky method of applying a dark shade of lipstick.

One coat would be smeared generously with the mouth puckered to a soundless 'O'. Smudging it a bit by pressing a tissue paper to the mouth would follow. An imprint of the painted lips came off on the napkin, but this was better than having the lipstick smear a teacup or a wine glass. That was considered sacrilege for a lady.

Another coat of the crimson colour would be daubed, with extra attention paid to the cupid bow shape of the upper-lip. Lipstick bleeding into the corners of the mouth was checked instantly, with some more dabbing of the tissue. And the last step was the examination of the front teeth, to wipe out any stains that could have appeared there.

If there was still time, my mum applied some lipstick on my childish mouth also. The family joke was that it was the best way to make me shut up, because I would refuse to talk with the colour on my lips, answering only in monosyllables afterwards.

Last week I was babysitting my boisterous four-year-old niece. When all efforts to make her go to bed failed, I approached her with a tube of red lipstick.

"Why are you doing?" she asked.

"Say O," I instructed.

"My mummy says children cannot wear lipstick," she told me.

"They can wake-up with make-up," I said circling her mouth in red.

"Goose night," she lisped, giggling.

"Goose night," I mimicked.

Blush On

I don't remember exactly when I became aware of the fact that I could never successfully tell a lie.

I had no problem twisting the truth, per se. When I was in school, I was very capable of transferring the blame for any misdemeanours, onto one of my two hapless brothers.

I mean, why would I not like watching their ears getting boxed by our disciplinarian mother? It was definitely a more preferred option than being subjected to the agony myself.

But I could not do it because my face gave me away.

It is not that my nose twitched or eyes became shifty. I could consciously control those doubting gestures by staring vacantly into space. No, that was not the case. The problem was that whenever I lied, my entire visage got suffused in a dark shade of crimson. And there was nothing I could do to stop it. I would be caught out in a jiffy, and the scolding was instantaneous.

My friends and family soon utilised this automatic blushing system, which nature supplied me with like an unwanted baggage, as a sort of litmus test. If the authenticity of any incident or remark had to be checked, they simply put it thorough me. You know, like the blue paper turning red under acidic conditions, my face would do the needful.

Somewhere along the way I sensitised myself enough to figure out exactly when a blush was about to make its unexpected appearance.

The minute I was subjected to any kind of untruth, at the very onset, the tips of my earlobes would start to tingle. It was as if a lightening rod was being applied to it. This sensation, spreading to my temples, would generate a deep flush on my cheeks, making me resemble a ruddy-faced monkey.

Also, the same thing happened if I was exposed to too much sunshine, excessive heat, or unblinking stares, from friends and strangers alike. I learned to live with it and took appropriate steps to protect myself from such situations, as and when they presented themselves.

And then, most unwillingly, I stumbled into mid-life crisis, a time that I was quite unprepared for. It altered my personality, beyond recognition. The mood-swings fluctuated from one extreme to another and, forget others; even I found it difficult to live with myself. There were days when I contemplated running away from home, but how could I hide from my own self?

The hot flushes were added fallout of this bewildering turn of events. I was used to blushing in shyness, embarrassment or untruthfulness, but this was like being in a state of constant blush. Unmindful of the weather conditions, I would break out into sweat, at the drop of a proverbial hat.

In sheer misery, I took to carrying folding-fans with me. I bought beautiful ones trimmed in Venetian lace, with pretty patterns on them. At the slightest excuse I would unfold one and wave it vigorously.

"Are you hot?" a suave gentleman asked me at a party recently.

"In my youth, or now?" I joked.

"Excuse me?" he was surprised.

"No," I clarified.

"I think not much has changed," he stated.

"Excuse me?" it was my turn to be startled.

"Since your younger days," he explained, smiling.

"The heat is making you blind," I muttered.

"And what is making you blush?" he queried.

"This lie detector test," I said, unfolding my hand-fan.

Acknowledgements

For every lazy columnist who is insulated in a cocoon of inertia, a veritable kick is needed to get them to assemble their work into a book form. These are some of the people who jolted me into activity with their continual encouragement, support and feedback.

Papa, Khuloud, Bishr, Rania, Abeer, Bunty, Geetan, Bikram, Rano, Gunit, Rahul, Maria, Jeff, JJ, Renee, Nadir, Meeta, Pavan, Vivek, Simi, Anurag, Raj, Ganesh, Didibhai, Farookh, Anu, Rishi, Soma, Vinni, Arindam, Rajat, Animesh, Radhika, Sanjay, Anjali, Sanjoy, Gautam, Tina, Sister Norella, Pawan, Babua, Om Uncle, Sandhu Aunty, Anil, Anupama, Harsh, Kikki, Raju, Arti, Bhaiya, Vannu, Manu, Ela, Piyoosh, Parinita, Sir Tony, Manjula, Ellie, Nikhil, Ishu, Varun, Nishu, Aanya and Ayan.

Special thanks to Nadira who urged me to write and sing and believe in myself.